Everything's Coming Up Clover

Dora Preston

ISBN: 149123802X
ISBN 13: 9781491238028
Library of Congress Control Number: 2013914429
CreateSpace Independent Publishing Platform
North Charleston, South Carolina

Foreword

I am delighted for the opportunity to introduce you to Clover, an irrepressible character brought to life through Dora's shrewd observations both as a care aide in a retirement community and as an advocate for the elderly. Clover is an oleo of some of the people Dora met during her many and varied interactions with other seniors both at work and at play. The exploits of her wickedly scheming yet naïve heroine resonate with the reality of the last chapters of life as Dora saw them.

While Dora herself had little in common with her cantankerous diva (she always saw the best in everyone and everything), her rich life experience shines through as her unique voice imbues Clover's adventures with sympathy, pathos and, above all, humour. The reader is never quite sure how it will all turn out but knows Clover will have the last word, and that there will likely be a sting in the tail.

Being one of the fortunate few who heard Dora read Clover's stories aloud I will always hear her delightful Yorkshire tones in my head as I read this book. And in my heart, always hold gratitude for her friendship.

Thanks to Dora's family for making Clover, and therefore Dora, always available to us, to lift our spirits, to make us laugh, but mostly to enable us to remember a remarkable woman.

Rosselind Sexton

ABOUT THE BOOK

Two years ago my mother, Dora Preston, was hospitalized with a ruptured appendix. Unfortunately her impending surgery revealed more. Yes, the appendix had ruptured. Regrettably, an undiagnosed tumour had also ruptured. Her diagnosis was bleak, and like her mother before her, we discovered that my mother was also to die from terminal colon cancer.

After the terrible news settled, my mother took stock. She had lived a life full of adventure, rich with love and laugher. But as a writer, there was an explicit regret. She revealed, "I wish I'd done more to publish my book." In fact, when her oncology appointment arrived, a close friend and I decided to attend, *hoping to soften the blow*. However, my mother had no intention of wallowing. Instead, once what we already knew was confirmed, my mother proceeded to explain to the doctors about her unpublished novel. With vigour and enthusiasm she launched into the story. The doctors sat patiently, intently listening as my mother gave an account of Clover's adventures and how Clover had arrived on the page. An hour later, still giggling about Clover, and Dora's insatiable determination, my friend and I wheeled her back to her hospital room.

Dora spent roughly ten years compiling the manuscripts that created *Everything's Coming Up Clover*. Its pages are filled with her many years of insight, wisdom and humour, crafted together by an amazing gift for writing. I am filled with enormous pride, and eternally grateful and honoured to bring this book to life for my mother. With peace and love, Mum, I fulfil a writer's final wish.

June 21st, 2011 one day short of her 85th birthday, my mother drew her final breathe.

Thank you for sharing the journey.
Glenys Preston Blackburn

Prologue

THIS DAY WILL GO DOWN IN INFAMY; I'LL SEE THAT IT DOES!

I've decided to write a diary so the world will know. Yes, they'll read how my two daughters and two sons had me incarcerated. How they've put their mum away in the prime of her life. How they've had her locked up in an 'old folk's home.' It was Horace, the eldest, who lowered the boom.

"We've been thinking, Mum," he said. "You've been doing some funny things lately...you know...forgetting stuff." He looked at the other three for help; they were only too willing to oblige. Muriel stopped polishing my TV screen with a paper towel and said,

"The manager tells us you keep losing your keys." I told her he was a snitch. I didn't tell them that yesterday I even lost the building. Then Doris started.

"You've done some very dangerous things, Mum. You've burned the ironing board right through, and how many times have we come in and turned the oven off?" I thought to myself, no wonder every time they come to see me I wind up with cold bed socks. I told them all to mind their own business and leave my oven alone. Fred, my youngest, had to join in, of course.

"Well, we wondered what on earth you were cooking, Mother. It smelled awful."

"Not half as bad as your wife's sauerkraut," I pointed out. Fred was quiet for a while and then he started again. He went on about the Halleluiah Chorus CD he and his wife Gerty bought me for Christmas. They caught me using it for a beer coaster.

"Well," I told him, "you can't sing along to a thing like that. I asked you for Tony Bennett. I didn't want a bunch of people singing at a funeral."

They all sat staring around the room for a while. Then Muriel went back to polishing the TV screen. She must have used at least half my roll of paper towels. It was my nice roll too, all covered with little butterflies! I only keep it for show. I was going to say something about it to Muriel when Doris suddenly started crying.

"Look at that lovely rubber plant me and Tom bought you." She blew her nose and sniffled a bit. "Do you think it's happy holding up all those Christmas ornaments?" I told her I didn't know. I never asked it. Then Muriel, from behind the pile of paper towels, noticed something else.

"I don't seem to recognize this pile of laundry here, Mother." She was sorting the clothing on the end of the coffee table. "Jockey shorts? And what are you doing with a T-shirt that says 'I spent a night with The Living Dead'?" I explained carefully how I forgot which dryer I was in.

"You're young," I told her, "wait till it happens to you."

"I'm fifty-six," she said and like Doris she started crying. Then Horace informed me about the plot they'd hatched for the New Year.

"Look, Mum, we've found a nice place, Honeystone Mansion. It's right downtown where you always like to be."

"Honeystone?" I shouted, "I've seen the people coming out of there. They're old!"

"You're nearly eighty, Mother," Doris said rolling her eyes. Only a young person of fifty-four could be so malicious and cruel. Horace told them all to shut up.

"We've been to see them at Honeystone Mansion; it's a lovely place," he insisted. "They tell us you can come and go as you please, and you know you love wandering around town." Then Fred piped up.

"It's for your own good, Mother."

"You're just a baby," I snapped. "What do you know?"

So they made up their minds. They're putting their old mother out to pasture. The van comes tomorrow to take all my treasured possessions to some auction. All those nice gramophone records of 'Wartime Melodies,' my 'Sing-a-long with Max Bygraves,' and my great big toffee tin full of buttons saved since I was a child. Two hundred and forty-seven Legion magazines; I marked a page in two of them where my husband was mentioned. I've got a fancy spoon collection from all the holidays he took me on. We were married forty-five years. Granted, there are only three spoons, but they're precious. And that lovely ball of string I've saved it since World War ll. I'm not sure why they asked us to save string–it's as big as a melon now. I hold the door back with it on a warm day. Will I need my husband's cricket bat anymore? I was waiting for a burglar, but one never came. The only piece of crockery I'm bothered about is grandma's old chamber pot. You can't replace treasures like that. It looked lovely last spring full of tulips.

I'll go to this Honeystone Mansion, but I won't make it easy for them. I know that!

DIARY OF CLOVER RAYTON

Honeystone Mansion

January

Jan. 5th

So this is Honeystone Mansion. I can't believe I have to sleep here tonight. I know I'm going to hate it. All four of them have just left. Oh, sure, they were slobbering a bit but it didn't stop them. They've checked me into 'Heartbreak Hotel,' and chopped me off at my golden years. Life as I know it is over!

Jan. 6th

Sandy, my grandson, came to see me today. I feel a lot better now. Sandy is eighteen and the son of Fred and Tilly. He's one of my favourites.

"Grandma," he said, "I know you want to keep a diary, so I've brought this little machine to save your wrist. It'll be much better than writing everything down. It'll record everything. Just tell it what you do each day, Grandma, and then they'll realize you're not crazy. You're just…you. And every now and then I'll get your words typed up for future generations to read." It sounds like some kind of magic to me, but I like it. I'll try to remember to talk to it just before I go to sleep each night.

Jan. 8th

This morning some young girl who said she was a care aide came in and reeled off a lot of instructions.

"My name is Rhodena. At meal times you go down the hall to your right where you will find the elevator, press the button with the arrow that points down, then, when you get on the elevator, press the button that says 'lobby.' The dining room is on your left. Honeystone Mansion has six floors and you are on the fourth. All the floors are colour coded. You are blue."

"You can say that again," I told her, "and do I have to do this load of rigmarole every time I eat?"

"You will catch on. Oh," she went on, "I also have to tell you, we have an open door policy."

"You mean you leave the doors open all the time?"

"No," she replied. "It means you can come and go as you please." With that she clipped a plastic bracelet round my wrist. 'Clover Rayton - Honeystone Mansion,' it says. There's also a phone number and an address.

"We do not want to lose you," she told me.

She sounded quite sincere actually.

Jan. 9th

Rhodena formally introduced me to the woman who shares this double room; her name is Maisey Polkinghouse. I disliked her on sight. Our beds are separated by a curtain. They're trying to kid us that we're in two rooms instead of one. Maisey stays in bed nearly all the time. It might be because whenever she gets up she falls down, so she has to get back in bed again. It's just an excuse to lie around, if you ask me. I can only see her head and shoulders most of the time. She looks like a sea lion with a white curly wig and a frilly collar. As soon as Rhodena had gone Maisey Polkinghouse proceeded to lay down the law.

"As you can see, we share the bathroom. The blue plastic dish is for my teeth. You use the green one."

Well, I thought, if that's the way she wants it, we'll soon see who's boss.

Jan. 10th

The registered nurse on the fourth floor is called Judy. She brought the house doctor, Dr. Harrison, to see me today. He seemed in a hurry. He asked a couple of questions like, was I suffering any pain anywhere?

"Yes," I said, "if you count the pain of a broken heart." He wrote something down on a chart and looked at the nurse.

"Usual stuff," he said. "A bit of heart trouble. Any S.O.B.?" he asked the nurse. I replied for her.

"Only my son Horace."

"The doctor means shortness of breath, Clover," Judy said, smiling sweetly.

"I know that," I said. The doctor handed the chart to the nurse and headed for the door, then turned and smiled.

"I'm sure we'll see each other often."

"Don't count on it," I told him.

Jan. 14th

Maisey Polkinghouse is stealing my stuff! So far I've lost two side combs, a bottle of camphorated oil, a bag of Licorice All Sorts, and a whalebone corset.

Jan. 17th

I know I'm not exactly as gorgeous as Marilyn Monroe. Fortunately the men of my age are getting a bit short-sighted so the odd flaw doesn't bother them. I could tell that I still had the 'touch' when a man walked into my room today.

"Hello," he said. "I'm the reception committee." I put down my *National Enquirer*. I looked into the bluest eyes I'd ever seen. The rest of him wasn't so hot. "Arthur Proctor's the name," he went on. "Seducing's the game."

I somehow knew he wasn't a member of the staff. He was about my age for one thing. His red plaid shirt was half in and half out of his baggy jogging pants. He was wearing a nice green silk tie though. His hair looked as if he had cut it himself without the use of a mirror. Or perhaps he meant every few strands to be different lengths. He picked up my hand and gave it a wet kiss.

"How could I have missed a beautiful woman like you?" He lowered his hand. It wafted down my chest and landed in my lap. I picked it up and handed it back to him.

"My name is Clover, but don't think you can walk all over me," I told him.

"I will see you anon," he said bowing. "That's Shakespeare you know, so au revoir, which of course is French, and goodbye." He shuffled out of the room. I liked his 'devil may care' manner. Maybe it won't be so bad here.

Maisey my roommate had to spoil things a bit though; her voice came over the partition separating us. "I see that old letch Arthur Proctor's been and tried it on with you."

I detected a note of jealousy. Women like me have to expect that.

Jan. 20th

Today I thought I'd check out this open door policy they keep talking about. I went to look at my old apartment building. I couldn't understand why it had moved. Then I realized I was lost. It was beginning to get dark when I found it. I thought I might have liked to go inside and look at my old apartment, but then I realized this isn't my home any more.

I turned back; I wanted so much to see a friendly face. I broke into a trot as I saw Clive, the evening care aide coming toward me. He was pushing a wheelchair.

"I knew where you'd be. Come on, your carriage awaits," he said as he kissed me. He covered my knees with a small quilt.

"How did you know where I'd be?" I asked him.

"Everyone goes back home at least once. You and me are going back to your new home; we'll have a nice cup of cocoa…alright?"

It was raining. I had my slippers on and no coat. I forgot it was January.

"Right," I said.

Jan. 22nd

Just when I had got used to finding the elevator and pressing the right button for the dining room, some man has offered to do it for me. He's a nice looking man, even though he's missing one leg. He said, "I pass your door each meal time. I'll call in, we can go down together." His artificial leg squeaks. This is good, I can hear him coming. It gives me chance to comb my hair and pick up my purse. He looks like what James Dean would have looked like if he'd lived to be in his seventies, got a haircut and smiled a bit. His name is Henry. I think that has a regal ring to it. He's younger than me, is seventy-six and that's all I look, on a good day!

Jan. 25th

I asked Maisey if she was going to Charlie Summersgill's birthday party today. "It's in the lounge at two," I said. "You know he's going to be ninety."

"Oh," said Maisey, "I thought you had to go to Buckingham Palace for that."

"For what?" I asked her.

"To be knighted," she said.

I swear all that falling down has damaged her eardrums.

Jan. 29th

I could have sworn I saw Maisey wearing my salmon pink sweater today. I knitted it myself in basket stitch. I looked in my clothes closet.

Lucky for her it was there.

February

Feb. 2nd

I called the police today; they came too. Well, one police-man came. He brought Judy the floor nurse with him. I told the young policeman they were abusing me. I told him everything. I asked him how he'd like to get bathed at six thirty in the morn-ing, with one little towel and a piece of motel soap. I said,

"I had twelve bottles of pills in this drawer. Do you see them now?" Judy admitted they'd been taken away.

"Some of the pills," she said, frowning at me, "were fifteen years old."

"I hope you're not going to steal everything I've got that's fifteen years old," I told her. "And another thing," I said, "who keeps stealing my partial denture and hiding it under the pil-low?" Judy smiled sweetly at the officer.

"We often find dentures under the pillow," she purred. She didn't fool the policeman though. When she'd gone he said,

"My grandmother is in a place like this and she tells me just the same things you do."

Feb. 12th

Rhodena got the dining room staff to put me and Henry at the same table. It's nice, we swap our food. I give him my sausages at breakfast and he gives me his eggs, half his pancake and the dish of maple syrup. At supper, I give him whatever I want to, but it's understood that I always get his dessert. He likes all the things I hate. I hate all the things he likes. We get along fine.

Feb. 13th

I asked Rhodena why I had to wear the plastic identity bracelet round my wrist.

"It gets caught on my sweater every time I put it on," I told her.

"Well, Clover," she explained, "you keep wandering away. I told you we do not want to lose you."

"I never go far," I said. She laughed and said, "Last night, Clover, the police brought you back from Seymour Street. You know those were prostitutes you were showing your family photos to?"

"I just stopped to admire the young woman's fishnet stockings, that's all," I told her.

"Another time, Clover," she went on, "the police brought you back because you were singing next to that awful man in the dirty raincoat, the one on Granville Street who uses two spoons to make music."

"Well, he needed help," I told her.

"He complained. He said you were driving away business, Clover. He wasn't tapping out the same song as you were singing."

"You know, Rhodena, I really feel my talents are completely wasted sometimes."

She hugged me and agreed.

Feb. 14th

It's Valentine's Day. Horace, Muriel, Doris and Fred, and their spouses, came today. Also, a couple of relatives I'd forgotten about. They all drifted in at different times of the day. Some of them found me, some of them didn't. The people who missed me left Valentine chocolates on my bed. I got seven heart-shaped boxes of chocolates. They're lacking a bit in imagination, I think. I'm glad my grandson Sandy found me; he never leaves until he does. He gave me six red roses. I know he got them from the vase at the front desk, but it's the thought that counts. At suppertime Henry moulded my mashed potatoes into the shape of a heart. I told him about the chocolates on my bed. He's coming to see them this evening.

This has been one of the nicest Valentine Days I can remember.

Feb. 16th

I left a couple of my boxes of chocolates by accident on the windowsill. The radiator is just under there, and they melted. It didn't matter though, me and Henry spread some of the chocolate on our breakfast toast this morning and it was great. The maraschino cherry ones were especially nice. I might melt some more chocolates.

Feb. 19th

There was a lot of noise outside my window today. I overlook the back alley of Honeystone Mansion. When I looked out I saw dozens of people down there. Several of them were sitting in canvas chairs that had letters written on the back. Bright lights were shining down from high posts. Several people were moving a big camera around. It was mounted on a platform. Quite a few people were standing around a stall set up with food and drinks. What a funny place to have a picnic, I thought.

The noise, I realized, was caused by a big red truck. A nice looking, blonde, young man was driving it up and down the alley. He kept speeding as far as Bute Street at the end of the alley, that's about two hundred yards away, and then he would screech to a stop. A man with a foghorn kept yelling at him to come back and do it again. Each time, the young man would back the truck up to just below my window and off he'd go again.

It was time to intervene.

"What are you doing?" I shouted through the window.

"A movie," someone shouted up to me. I went back to reading my copy of the *Superior Senior's Magazine*. I tried to get interested in a very nice article. It was about a ninety-two year old woman. She had been potting mums for twenty years. She had four hundred and twenty-seven flower pots in the back yard. Unfortunately the police found that she was getting the mums from Stanley Park. This is the sort of human-interest stuff I usually enjoy. However, all the time I was reading, I was aware of this truck stopping and starting under my window. The man with the foghorn wasn't helping either. I had to put a stop to this. I leaned out of the window. The young man was hanging out of the truck window. I thought to myself, a handsome young man like this should not be riding up and down an alley in a battered, old, red truck; he should be in the park with some nice young woman. Foghorn was shouting through a large, cone-shaped thing.

"It's getting better, Mac. Do it again." Mac needed some guidance, I thought.

"Listen Mac," I shouted. "If you can't drive that bloody truck, leave it alone." The young man grinned up at me. Foghorn looked around at a group of people standing close by. In a rather bad-tempered voice he said,

"Do something about the old girl, will ya?"

"Hey," I yelled, "I live here. You're just borrowing the alley." Half an hour later things quieted down. I was now reading an informative article on bladder control. I got to the part where it told me how many times through the night one should have to go pee. Three seemed to be the consensus. I know now why a lot of folks here are told to wear grown-up diapers. It also dawned on me what all the ripping and tearing noises are that I hear through the night. It's Maisey doing night time trips to the bathroom. I thought it was mice!

A knock on the door interrupted me. I'd left it partly open as usual. Someone was standing there. It was Foghorn. He handed me a large box of chocolates.

"Sorry about the noise," he said. "We're filming. You'll see it later on TV. We're just wrapping up."

"Oh, I thought maybe that young man had run out of gas," I said.

"No. We've finished shooting," he told me.

"I felt like doing some shooting of my own," I replied. He smiled; he had a really nice smile. A terrible voice, but a nice smile. He was American, of course.

I told Foghorn, "This has been a great month for chocolates."

Feb. 21st

I had a strange experience today. Two old ladies came tripping into my room. I'm sure there were two of them, unless I was having an optical illusion. They were absolutely identical, about five feet tall, with white curly hair. They had little red mouths and really pink cheeks. Their dresses had frills round the hem. They reminded me of two large dolls that could walk. Both of them stood smiling down at me. Then they spoke as though they'd been programmed. The first one said, "Hello, I'm Felicia."

"Hello, I'm Selicia," said the other one.

"We live here." They said this simultaneously. It was incredible! I told them I was called Clover. They both broke into song as they took tiny steps backward to the door.

"I'm looking over a four-leafed clover…" their voices disappeared down the hall. I called Rhodena, the care aide.

"I need my eyes tested, Rhodena," I told her, "I'm seeing double."

"No, no," she laughed, "you just saw the twins. The other residents call them the Dolly Sisters. They're funny." She made circles at the side of her forehead with one finger. I think all over the world this means the same thing…the twins are identically dotty.

Feb. 23rd

I never knew anyone who could fall as often as my roommate Maisey. She fell again today. But of all the inconsiderate places to fall, her head and shoulders were blocking the door into the hall. Worse still, her legs were across the bathroom door. I rang the bell of course, and Rhodena came. She tapped on the door then tried to push it open. But Maisey's head was in the way. I was just a second too late warning Rhodena to be careful. Poor Maisey got whacked. Rhodena slipped her hand through the narrow opening and patted Maisey's head.

"I will get help." I then heard Rhodena hurrying down the hall. Maisey just moaned. I needed to go to the bathroom at this point. I nearly got a hernia bending Maisey's legs so that I could squeeze through the bathroom door. When I finished, I put a pillow under Maisey's head, then threw a cardigan over her and told her,

"Think of this as nap time." I then went back to watch 'Coronation Street.' It must have been only ten minutes later when I heard a noise at the door. Two great big firemen climbed in. They picked Maisey up as though she was a baby and set her on her bed. She'd fallen asleep. Rhodena rushed over to Maisey beaming. The nurse came in with a tray full of tea and stuff. Then the doctor came. They all messed about for ages taking Maisey's blood pressure and everything. I was totally ignored.

No wonder Maisey falls a lot!

Feb. 24th

Maisey is having her meals in bed for a few days. I've decided to stop pinching her blue dish, the one she likes for her teeth. I'll stick to the green one. Anyone off balance enough to fall all over like she does doesn't need any more confusion. I shared Foghorn's chocolates with her. I even showed her how to make my secret chocolate spread.

Feb. 25th

Me and Henry keep getting trapped in the elevator with someone we call 'Frankenstein's Monster.' This man is seven feet tall if he's an inch! He has a red scar across his forehead and down one side of his face. Rhodena tells me he's had brain surgery. No one has ever heard him speak a word. I'm not afraid of him; it's just that he always does the same thing. He lumbers onto the elevator and presses every single button, six, five, four, three, two, then the lobby and then the alarm. He lives on the fourth floor like me and Henry. Thank God there are only six floors in the whole building. When we finally get off the elevator my stomach feels as though it's trying to get past my tonsils. We then have the embarrassment of walking through a crowd of people. They always ask, what's the emergency? If there are any relatives in the group, they're bound to wonder what kind of death trap they've put their folks into.

Feb. 27th

Maisey is well enough to go down to the dining room now. That's if she can keep on her feet. She thanked me for all I'd done for her. I forgot to keep putting in my diary that I brought her a cup of tea from the kitchen a couple of times a day. I'm going to be nicer to her family when they come. I won't get them in the hall and tell them she's at death's door anymore. I'll tell them I'm going to help her get through. I hope they don't misunderstand.

March

Mar. 2nd

I got myself in trouble today, all because of doing someone a good turn. Monster lives two doors down the hall from me and Maisey. Today I saw him standing outside his room crying and beating his head against the door. He was locked out. I know what it feels like to be locked out. Well, with me, it was more like I'd lost my keys and couldn't get in. But it's the same feeling. Monster needed help. The residents here hardly ever lock their doors. They don't give us any keys. When anyone goes to hospital or dies I've noticed Rhodena and the other care aides lock the door with a master key. Then I've watched as they hang the key by the medicine cupboard at the nursing station.

No one was around, so I pinched the key. I opened the door for him and strange fumes hit me as soon as we got through the door. Monster wiped his eyes on his shirtsleeve as he shambled into the room. I was curious to know what his room looked like so I followed close behind. As usual, he never said a word. Suddenly, he turned and we collided. He went down on his knees, which made him just the same height as me. His glazed eyes looked into mine then he keeled over sideways.

It was then that I noticed dozens of tiny insects on the bed and the floor. They were lying on their backs, their little legs pointing up toward the ceiling. Was this like the elephants in the jungle? The way they travelled to some secret place to die? Was this where all the little insects came to end their days? I too had a terrible urge to die...well, at least fall asleep. As I slumped on top of Monster the last thing I thought was, I hope Henry and my family understand.

I woke up in the emergency unit at St. Paul's Hospital. A white-coated man was leaning over me.

"Poor old woman," I heard him say. "You'd think they'd lock the residents' doors when they fumigate their rooms, wouldn't you?"

I pretended to be asleep.

Mar. 8th

This morning I couldn't get the bathroom light to go on. Fortunately, I had one of my Christmas candles left and a box of matches. I lit the candle and put it on the tank behind the toilet seat. Somehow, while I was comfortably sitting on the toilet, the silly candle fell onto the floor. It rolled just out of reach, so I dropped a face cloth on it hoping to kill the flame. I missed. A corner of the face cloth touched the candle and began to singe. Thinking quickly, I grabbed Maisey's underslip, which was hanging on the towel rack and tossed it on top of the face cloth. Then, for good measure, I tossed on Maisey's crinoline doll, the one she'd knitted herself that covers the spare toilet roll. The last thing I added to the pile was Maisey's *Little Book of Prayers*, which is always beside the toilet seat. This was a mistake. God was watching. The whole pile smoked, and then glowed. I went as fast as I could into the hall yelling "Fire, fire, my bathroom's on fire."

Rhodena seemed to have trouble believing I had set fire to the bathroom.

"The bathroom!" she exclaimed. "How can fire be in the bathroom?"

"Easy," I shouted. "Come and see." Rhodena grabbed the fire extinguisher from the wall behind the nursing station. I thought, good, I've always wanted to know how those things work. Leo, who cleans the floors, put his mop into his bucket and followed. I called back to him,

"Phone the fire department, Leo, just in case." Our fourth floor nurse Judy came running, followed by some of the more agile residents.

"Keep calm, keep calm," Judy shouted as everybody piled into the bathroom. I pushed my way to the front; after all it was my fire. I noticed everyone had suddenly gone quiet, and then I saw why.

There was Maisey sitting on the toilet. She was in a slight haze from the smoke and, as usual, seemed to have no idea what was going on. She looked quite nice really. There was a rosy glow all around her. She had just pulled off about a yard of toilet paper. She looked at us quite mystified. The paper fell from her hand. It floated as though drawn by a magnet to the nice little fire at the back. Maisey's mouth opened to speak but nothing came.

"Squirt it. Squirt it," I shouted at Rhodena who was dodging back and forth with the extinguisher. She was trying to get a bead on the fire without hitting Maisey. Everyone shouted instructions. I got impatient and went to my dresser for the jug of ice water. I pushed to the front again and flung it. A lot went on Maisey, I admit, but some of it went on the fire.

"There, you see?" I said to Rhodena. "That's how you put a fire out!" I nudged her to make my point clear. She staggered back over someone's foot, and the top of the fire extinguisher came off. Soapy spray flew everywhere. It looked as though a bomb had hit a barber's shop. The front of Judy's hair had turned white, her eyes were narrow slits. She seemed to be groping for someone, I wasn't sure who.

Rhodena struggled to stop more spray from coming out of the extinguisher, but it seemed to make it splatter more. Always ready in an emergency, I quickly got the quilt from my bed and threw it over Rhodena and the extinguisher. It was then we heard the siren.

"Firemen are coming, firemen are coming." Leo stood beaming in the doorway. Everyone scattered. I steered Rhodena into the hall. She managed to punch her way out of the quilt. Rhodena ran with Judy down the hall to the elevator, bits of froth dancing off both of them. I was left alone with Maisey; she looked very messy and very sad.

"Well," I said, "Kay ser rah, ser rah. Which means, never go into a bathroom when it's on fire." I spent a lovely half hour explaining to the wonderful young firemen how it all happened. I have to say they seemed as mystified as Maisey.

Not everybody can be as in charge of the situation as I always am.

Mar. 9th

Rhodena came and forgave me for nearly suffocating her with my quilt. Maisey is not speaking to me, again. Considering I probably saved her life, that's ingratitude. Judy came to see me. I didn't like her attitude, but then I never do.

"The fire department is coming to give us a lecture," she said. She looked at my wet comforter and glanced at the mess in the bathroom. "They will speak on the correct procedure when dealing with a fire. I would certainly hope, Clover, that you will be there."

"I think I have proved conclusively that I can deal with a fire." I said humbly. "In fact I could give a lecture."

Judy left muttering something about an early retirement.

Mar. 10th

A weird little man came to see me today. He weighed about ninety pounds and all of it in a tizzy. He held a notebook and pencil. He kept waving them both at me and doing a little dance at the same time.

"My name is Snerd," he said. "I'm the cost clerk. I've come to assess the damage perpetratcd in here." He pointed with his pencil to the bathroom. He did a little side step, keeping his beady eyes on me. He waved the book back and forth like a matador in a bullring. When he disappeared into the bathroom I picked up my large print *Reader's Digest* and settled back to read. The article said that the slowest drivers were old people. I was just contemplating how bad it would be if we drove fast, when I heard Snerd scream at the top of his voice.

"My God," he shouted.

"What's the matter," I asked, "haven't you seen a bit of blistered paint before?" He came dancing over to me, dropping a piece of black rag at my feet.

"One face cloth costing two fifty," he snapped, scribbling furiously in his notebook. Then, pointing the pencil about an inch from my nose, he shrieked, "Ruined!" He did his sidestep in and out of the bathroom again. "One undergarment costing at least twenty dollars," he shouted, dropping a crumpled black ball at my feet. How could he tell what it was, I thought, since it was ruined. Then he threw the charred remains of Maisey's crinoline doll on the floor.

"One irreplaceable piece of artwork, ruined." He said it as though I'd set fire to the Sistine Chapel. He came toward me holding his pencil like a bullfighter coming in for the kill.

He stopped dead when I said,

"By the way, did you see the quilt?" I pointed to it. I had draped it over the radiator. I didn't tell him I was just letting it dry.

"Don't tell me it's...?"

I said it with him, "Ruined." He tapped my shoulder with his pencil, and then he did a few jerky sidesteps to the outside door. He turned to me.

"How does the word firebug strike you, Madam?" He was holding the door open.

"How do the words bugger off strike you?" I asked.

"You're in trouble," Snerd muttered, poking his pencil at me through the doorway.

I walked over and grabbed hold of the end of the pencil. Then pushed the door shut, snapping the pencil in two.

Mar. 11th

Ms. McPherson is the head administrator over all of Honeystone Mansion (we call her the Big Boss). She doesn't often come on the floors, never mind into our rooms. She glides like a fairy godmother around the tables in the dining room and the lounge. Always smiling sweetly she kisses certain residents, depending on how long they've been here. I won't qualify for another few years. There are only two reasons why Ms. McPherson might come to your room. One is to tell you you're too sick to stay here at Honeystone and must go to a real nursing home. The other reason is you've broken a rule, of which I'll swear there's a thousand. In short, when you see Ms. McPherson upstairs on the floors, it means trouble.

She came to see me today. She wafted through the door and sat beside me on the bed. She arranged her dress around her as though posing for a portrait. I studied the quality of her clothes. They certainly didn't come from the Salvation Army. Ms. McPherson went on about the quality of life here at Honeystone Mansion. Then she said,

"Now, Mrs. Rayton, I've been getting complaints."

"Oh," I said, "you surprise me, you seem so perfect to me."

"No, no, no. I mean about you," she went on. "I believe Mr. Snerd–a very important member of our staff–came to see you yesterday. Now, um...Clover, may I call you Clover?"

"That's my name," I told her.

"Now, I believe..." she put her arm around my shoulder, "some bad language was used."

"You're darn right," I told her. "You should have heard him. I think he should be fired."

"Mrs. Rayton!" She pumped my bed with her fist. "We are at cross purposes here." She wiped a fleck of moisture from her chin with a small, lace-edged hanky, then, shaking a lovely manicured finger, she said, "I want you to promise that when you come into contact with Mr. Snerd again you will treat him in the manner he deserves. Is that understood?"

"Yes," I said, "he'll get just what he deserves."

Ms. McPherson got up quickly from the bed, which bounced, nearly toppling me over. She flounced through the door, slamming it behind her. Unfortunately, the bottom edge of her dress got caught in the door. Instead of opening the door and getting herself free, she tugged and tugged from the other side. I watched the expensive piece of silk fabric on my side of the door as it got smaller and smaller. Finally the dress ripped. A tiny coloured segment fell on my floor. It looked like a dead butterfly. I'm sure I heard her say, "Shit," as she hurried down the hall.

I think I'll send a letter to the board of governors. People like me who are old and helpless should not have to tolerate all this bad language from tyrannical and oppressive administration staff.

Mar. 20th

Maisey's wig accidentally got sent down the laundry chute with her clothes. It came back yesterday in tatters, but she still insists on wearing it. I like it! She looks like a raccoon that's just stepped on a live voltage wire.

Mar. 31st

Today, me and Henry were sitting in the lounge on the main floor watching a show on our giant TV screen. It was about the propagation of porpoises. Mrs. Westby, who lives on the fourth floor like us, was sitting on the sofa beside us.

"You know, Henry," I said, "I don't know how a porpoise finds it, never mind knows what to do with it."

"Oh," Henry answered, "When you get the urge, you find it all right." Henry has a lovely way of putting things. I looked at Mrs. Westby for her input. She wasn't showing any interest in the porpoises. Her head looked uncomfortable. It was sort of lolling on one side.

"I don't think she's with us anymore," I told Henry.

"Wait till the tea trolley comes round," he said. "She'll come to life then." But she didn't. At three o'clock prompt, Kalmunder, the kitchen aide, came around as usual with tea. She handed a cup to Mrs. Westby who usually grabs it. I noticed Kalmunder's hand shaking. I grabbed the cup and saucer before she let it fall. Kalmunder ran to the nearest interphone. Me and Henry went back to the propagating porpoises. A bit later we heard the loud-speaker. We both strained to listen to the TV show, but we were vaguely aware of the loudspeaker, repeating over and over, "code blue...code blue. Lounge area..."

It wasn't long before the fourth floor nurse, Judy, appeared. She was closely followed by Bill and Sonny, the male care aides who had just come on duty for the three to eleven shift. Judy whispered out of the side of her mouth to the two young aides.

"Don't let the residents know anything's wrong." Smiling sweetly, which she's very good at, she leaned over Mrs. Westby. "Um...Mrs. Westby, how would you like to go upstairs for your bath? It's Tuesday you know...we've even brought a wheelchair for you."

"I don't think she cares what day it is," I told Judy. "She's dead." Bill and Sonny grinned. Judy straightened up, looking fiercely at me.

"For goodness sakes, keep quiet, Clover!" She gave Bill a nudge.

"Okay, now lift her quick." Bill and Sonny are both about five foot six and quite slender. They struggled and finally got the two hundred pound Mrs. Westby into the wheelchair.

Judy spoke loudly so everyone could hear. "That's it, Mrs. Westby, you're doing fine." Bill and Sonny were now struggling to get the old lady sitting as straight as possible.

"God, she weighs a ton," whispered Bill.

"Hurry up," said Judy, "everyone's watching."

"Tell me about it," muttered Sonny as he smoothed Mrs. Westby's dress and pulled up her knee-high stockings.

I was curious to know what the next move would be, so I asked Henry to wait for me while I followed the group out of the lounge. They headed to the front desk. Judy slapped her hand sharply on the counter.

"Quick, Diane, get her chart." She nodded at the slumped Mrs. Westby. "Look for the next of kin so we know which funeral home to send her to. We can't take her to her room. She shares it with that strange woman who believes in reincarnation or something." Diane got up from her chair and peered over the top of the counter.

"You mean she's...um...she's...um..."

"Dead," I told her.

"Do you mind, Clover?" Judy was tapping again on the counter. Diane had gotten Mrs. Westby's chart and was now dialling a number. Then we heard a one-sided conversation.

"Oh, no, you're kidding...Don't tell me."

"What? What?" asked Judy.

"The next of kin is her brother. He died two days ago!" Diane told her.

"I could have told you that," I piped up. "He owed her a lot of money. It looks as though she's going off where he's gone. Maybe she's going to track him down."

"Thanks for the information," snapped Judy. "I needed that."

The two aides were looking at each other. They both shrugged. Judy gave Bill a little push.

"Quick," she told him, "run to the basement and get a stretcher. We'll have to leave her overnight right here in Nellie's second-hand shop." She pointed to the clothes shop in between the reception desk and the administration office. Twice Upon a Time, the sign said over the door.

"Nellie's shop won't be open for business till Friday," Judy pointed out. "We've got two days. We'll get it all sorted out by then." Judy turned to Diane behind the desk. "Just tell the coroner where she is when he comes. Don't tell anyone else."

Bill soon got back with the stretcher. Judy reached out to Diane for the key to Nellie's shop. She opened the door to Twice Upon a Time.

"Okay," said Judy, as she followed Bill and Sonny who pushed the chair and the empty stretcher through the shop doorway. I could hear Judy's voice. "This is going to be a hell of a tussle. Now we've got to get her out of the chair and onto the stretcher. Thank God no one's going to see us in here."

"Tell us about it," said Sonny. I sat down and waited on the comfortable chair by the reception desk. The three of them came out a while later. Sonny was pushing the empty wheelchair. They looked as though they'd just run up ten flights of stairs.

Just as they were handing back the key to Diane, Nellie, who runs the second-hand shop, came through the front door and up to the desk. Nellie's eighty-two years old. She looks every minute of it but she's too busy to die. Nellie also runs the candy shop and takes both her jobs very seriously.

"Oh, Nellie," said Judy. "We've just had to put a cadaver in your shop. I hope you don't mind?"

"That's fine. That's fine," said Nellie. "As long as you've had it dry cleaned and written the size on it." Judy looked at Bill and Sonny.

"God, I don't believe this. Let's go, I've had enough."

"Tell us about it," said Sonny.

April

April 1ˢᵗ

It's April first. I know because my grandson Sandy just called.

"Hey, Grandma," he said, "the Martians have landed."

"Don't worry," I told him, "they'll take forever to get through customs and security."

"You've spoiled my April Fool thing," Sandy said, "but I still love ya."

After Sandy hung up, I got to remembering what fun it was as a child to wake up on the morning of April first. I'd think to myself, now who can I make a fool of? But, I also knew the rule was, you couldn't make anyone an April Fool after twelve noon. It was ten o'clock. I decided to go see Nellie at the candy shop.

When I got there I said, "Nellie, you know how I'm always giving you stuff for your Twice Upon a Time shop? All those things my two daughters keep bringing me?"

"Yes," she said, "but I don't get to keep all the money you know, Clover. Seventy-five cents on the dollar goes for gas for all those bus trips you keep going on."

"I know that," I said, "but you get all the glory."

"What do you want, Clover?" she snapped.

"I want that nice gray pullover, the one I brought you the other day. I want it for Henry."

"Why can't you wait until Friday when the store opens?"

"Someone might get it before me. Come on Nellie," I pleaded. "You've got your own key. I'll look after the candy shop till you come back."

"Seems to me you could wait just two more days," she grumbled.

"I'll give you twice what you were asking," I offered. "What were you asking, by the way?"

"Five seventy-five," she answered. I knew for a fact it was only five dollars but I never argued.

She finally gave in and left for the clothes shop. I was left to mind the candy store. I enjoyed myself for a while. I got all the latest gossip from the customers that came. Then I began to wonder why Nellie was taking so long. I thought she'd be back in five minutes and then I'd say, "April Fool," and we'd have a good laugh and that would be it. I got stuck in that candy shop two whole hours. I was fed up. I ate two Mars bars, a Snickers bar and a bag of chips. I was feeling sick by lunchtime. I began to realize that this was no fun and I'd better go investigate.

When I got to Nellie's second-hand store, the Dolly Sisters, who are identically crazy, were standing with their ears against the door of the shop. Several other residents had joined them. I noticed Diane leaning over the reception counter watching them all.

"What is it?" Diane called out to them.

"Someone's moaning," one of the twins told her.

"What?" shrieked Diane.

"And scratching," said the other sister.

"That's impossible," said Diane. Everyone looked puzzled as Diane, in a shaky voice, said over the intercom on her desk, "Judy... Judy...code blue...code blue... Twice Upon a Time...code blue..." Just then, Ms. McPherson appeared from her office. She looked at the half dozen residents standing by the door of the second-hand shop.

"Why are you congregating here?" she asked in her very refined voice. At that moment, Judy and four care aides came running out of the elevator. The moaning and scratching was growing louder.

"Someone wants to get out." It was the twins again.

"They certainly mean to get out." The Dolly Sisters nodded their heads in unison like wind up dolls. Ms. McPherson shouted,

"Is there something I should know, Judy? Exactly what is going on?" Judy's hand covered her eyes as she said,

"It's Mrs. Westby. We'd nowhere else to put her. She's...she's.... dead." Something seemed to hurl itself at the door of the shop as Judy spoke. Ms. McPherson turned and faced the crowd that had now gathered.

"I want everyone who isn't staff to move back." Everyone stepped about six inches backward. Ms. McPherson's face was white as she put her hand on the doorknob and turned it. She tried to push back the door but something was behind it. Then, a hand appeared around the door followed by a white face. A gray wig had somehow turned sideways, making the head appear to have screwed itself around. Everyone gasped as the apparition opened its mouth to speak.

"I...was locked in with...with...." She pointed behind her as she tottered forward into Ms. McPherson's arms. The door of the shop slowly closed behind her, but not before everyone caught a glimpse of a white-draped figure lying on a stretcher.

"Who was that?" asked one of the Dolly Sisters.

"All in white," said the other one.

I decided I'd better say something. "Well, it was supposed to be an April Fool joke," I told them.

"April who?" asked one of the twins.

"Do we know her?" asked the other.

Ms. McPherson passed Nellie over to Judy. She turned and glowered at me. Now, realizing who it was that had emerged from the shop, everyone began milling around Nellie and asking questions. I decided to leave quickly. I hurried back to the candy store. I realized that Nellie wouldn't be back for a while. I picked up all the empty candy wrappers and undid a new box of chocolate bars. I dusted the shelves. Then I put up the *CLOSED* sign.

After all, what are friends for?

April 6th

I went to find the cook today. She's not really the cook. Lorylee is filling in for Sidney who is an excellent cook. Sidney will be gone for a little while; he had to go to the east coast on family business. Actually he's been charged with bigamy, so there's more than one family business to deal with. We all wish he'd get back soon. I found the so-called cook, all three hundred pounds of her, hunched over her lunch in the staff room.

"Lorylee," I said. "I'd like to talk to you about those miniature bombs you keep serving in the morning. Boiled eggs, I think you call them." She was just opening the box in front of her. 'Harry's Pizza,' it said on the lid. "I see you've got a lot of faith in your own cooking," I said as I sat beside her. I reached for a slice of pizza and she slapped my hand.

"Well, what about the eggs?" she asked with her mouth full of food.

"Have you ever thought of selling them to some arms manufacturer?" I asked. "They'd be more deadly than a hand grenade," I said.

"I don't know what you're worrying about," she shot back. "Everyone knows you old people have no taste buds left. They're dying off, same as your faculties."

"Well," I answered, "if I was a taste bud, I'd shrivel up and die at the sight of your cooking. By the way, next time you go for a pizza, bring Harry back with you. Maybe we can get him to cook for us." I quickly picked up a slice of pizza and headed for the door.

April 11th

Because of the unfortunate Mrs. Westby incident, as Ms. McPherson keeps calling it, the office staff has made up a form; they're calling it a funeral form. We have to get our families to fill out a questionnaire about what our funeral arrangements are, and which funeral home we will go to when we 'lose our mortal coil,' as Shakespeare would say.

Rhodena took me along to Judy at the nursing station. She suggested to Judy that I would be a good person to take the forms to each room on the fourth floor.

"Well," said Judy, "she's partly responsible for all this extra red tape, so maybe she should do it."

"It is just that she knows everybody," said Rhodena. "The residents listen to her."

"Unfortunately, you're right, Rhodena," said Judy, as she handed me a pile of forms.

"Remember, Clover, just leave the forms on the dressers in the residents' rooms. Don't make any suggestions...it's up to the family what happens to them when they die, not you!"

"I don't need anyone to tell me about diplomacy, Judy," I told her. "And, in case you don't know, I'm a member of the Problem Solving Committee, so I intend to combine this funeral job with my problem stuff. By the way," I asked, "you don't need this done in a hurry, do you?"

"No," said Judy. "Make the job last for as long as possible. While you're doing that, you're not doing...other things. And I'm glad to know you're solving problems, Clover. I thought perhaps you were just creating them." She hurried away before I could say anything.

I thought to myself, there's gratitude after all I've done around here!

April 13th

I was glad to start my funeral form deliveries today. I needed something to cheer me up. They've taken Henry to the hospital at the university. They're going to examine his leg; well, what's left of it, that is.

April 19th

Lorylee, the cook from Hell, called me over today.

"Clover," she said, "with regard to our conversation the other day about the boiled eggs you get twice a week..."

"Yes, have you found a solution?" I asked.

"I think I have," she said. There was something fishy about her. She was being too nice.

"What I'm going to do is this," she went on. "I'll put your initials on your egg with a marker pen. Then I'll fish your egg out first, how's that?"

"Sounds like a good idea," I told her.

April 20th

That rat Lorylee put my initials on my egg alright. She must have dipped it into the water then lifted it right out again. I took the top off and slimy goo dribbled all over my lap.

This means war!

April 23rd

I was awakened this morning by a strange sound in the alley. I looked down and just below my window I saw a large dog. It was attempting to free itself from its leash, which seemed to be caught on something. The poor thing was whining pitifully. Being the dog lover I am, I quickly dressed and went down.

The dog wagged its tail when it saw me. It was a breed I didn't recognize. All I knew was that it needed help. I soon discovered the problem. The leash was caught under the wheels of our big garbage container. It took me a minute or two to get it free. I couldn't read the collar tag without my glasses but I could see that the dog was panting because it needed a drink.

"I wonder if you're a boy or girl," I said. Immediately it lifted its leg and peed on the garbage container as if to say, there, does that answer your question? This dog is very bright I thought as I took up the end of the leash.

"We'll go up to my room and I'll get you a nice bowl of water, eh?" When I tugged at the leash the dog resisted. "What's up?" I asked. The dog pointed with its nose at something half under the garbage bin. I bent down to look. It was a dead rat. As much as I tried to pull the dog away, he remained still. "Well," I said, "I guess it's your trophy and you want to keep it."

I looked around and on the top of the bin someone had placed all the newspapers from the day before. I laid several of them on the ground and picked up the rat by the tail. When I had finished it was nicely wrapped up. It reminded me of a parcel of fish and chips. They were always served in newspaper like this when I was a girl. I put the package under my arm and pulled at the leash. This time the dog understood that the rat was coming along too.

We managed to get through the back door and up to the fourth floor without being seen. The only sound had come from the cooking of breakfast in the kitchen. The dog seemed to like my room. It explored underneath my bed and came out with its nose covered in dust. It then put its paws on my windowsill and finished off a saucer of leftover Valentine chocolates.

I put the rat under my dresser and filled my fruit bowl with water. The dog had a good long drink then sat and licked its paws and stomach. I liked having a pet. I decided to show him to Henry and thought we could take it for a walk. I put my glasses on and read its nametag. 'Attila the Hun,' it said.

I checked the hallway for staff. They have very narrow views on the kinds of things we keep in our rooms. They had quickly gotten rid of Ken Selecar's python and I remember the fuss they made about Arthur Proctor's tarantula.

I couldn't see anyone in the hall so I led Attila toward Henry's room, just six doors away. However, we'd only gone two steps when the dog stopped. It had heard something. The one person in the whole world I didn't want to meet was creeping up behind us. It was Snerd, Snerdy Turdy, as I had decided to refer to him. I thought the name suited him perfectly. He had never forgiven me for the insignificant little fire that scorched a few things in my bathroom. His skinny little frame was all aquiver.

"You've done it this time, Clover," he snarled. Then he danced a little closer. He took a good look at the dog and his expression changed to shock and fear. "Get that thing out of here immediately. Do you hear?" he growled.

"Keep your shirt on," I told him. "I'm just taking it out for a walk."

"Do you know what that thing is?" he shouted.

"Well, let me guess," I replied. "It has four legs." I pretended to count them. "It goes 'woof woof' so I guess it's a dog. Do I get a prize?"

"It's a pit bull!" Snerd was frothing at the mouth. I could feel the dog tensing up beside me.

"It's not any kind of a bull, silly," I said. "It's a dog." Snerd pointed at the dog's face.

"This..." he said, his finger shaking close to the dog's nose, "is a dangerous animal." He continued to poke his finger closer and closer to the dog's face. "These dogs," he went on, "are killers." Snerd's finger actually touched the dog. Attila must have remembered he hadn't had breakfast, because his teeth closed with a tiny click over Snerd's finger.

The scream brought people to their doors. They all wore different forms of night attire. Arthur Proctor came into the hall wearing his nightshirt; it was gray and fell past his knees. Someone had sewn a huge pocket eight inches by twelve in the middle at the front. The pocket was bulging and he looked like an albino kangaroo.

The Dolly Sisters arrived in matching frilly nighties.

"A doggy," said one of them.

"A doggy," said the other.

All this time Snerd was moving in little circles while holding his finger. He looked like a square dancer in pain, and was making noises like a badly tuned violin. No one paid him any attention.

"You are all witnesses," Snerd shouted, holding up his arm while still moving in circles. "I need the attention of a nurse. Quick, someone get me a nurse." One or two people looked casually around, but no one moved. Clive, the night care aide, came from behind the desk down the hall with his leather jacket slung over his shoulder. He was going off duty, but he stopped to say goodbye.

"What are you doing, Mr. Snerd? Why are you doing a heil Hitler?" Clive came over and patted the dog's back. Snerd held out his finger, his face screwed up like a little child's, babbling about the 'vicious dog.'

"I don't see anything," said Clive still patting the dog. "Oh, yes, there's a mark but there's no blood." Snerd angrily pulled his finger away.

"What kind of a care aide are you?" he said nastily.

"A bloody tired one," said Clive. "So long," he said and left. Everyone dispersed except me and Snerd. Attila had been enjoying the gentle patting and genial chatter from the residents and now clung to my side as we both faced our mortal enemy.

"I'll have that dog put down if it's the last thing I do," Snerd muttered and then stomped over to the elevator.

I was close to tears when Attila and I arrived at Henry's room. I realized as I entered how Henry always makes me feel better when I'm down, which isn't often. We left Attila eating a stale meat sandwich in Henry's room while we went for breakfast.

Afterward, me and Henry and Attila spent a few enjoyable hours in Stanley Park. We both knew we'd better look at the address on Attila's name tag though.

"Well, here goes," said Henry. He read the tag. "It's a posh address, Clover," he said. "It's in Shaughnessy. I guess we'll need help from the administration at Honeystone." When we returned and went through the front door, Ms. McPherson was talking to Diane at the desk. She suddenly stopped talking and beamed at us.

"Oh, here they come!" Ms. McPherson came to greet us as though we were royalty. She never actually smiles at me, so I was very surprised. Her eyes flicked nervously from us to the dog.

"So..." she said still beaming. "This is Attila? Mr. Snerd told me you were taking care of the dog for him." I was puzzled. Ms. McPherson explained. "Our president, Mr. Oppenheimer, left the dog in the activity room last evening, while he went to the Orpheum Theatre. He was devastated to find it gone when he got back."

"Yes and...?" I asked.

"Well, wasn't it clever of Mr. Snerd to find the dog and ask you both to take care of it for him? I think Mr. Snerd deserves every bit of the reward, don't you?"

"Oh, yes," said Henry, "we'll go and congratulate him right now."

"Where is Mr. Oppenheimer?" I asked.

"He's in Mr. Snerd's office," she answered. I took Henry's arm.

"Into the fray," I said, nodding at Ms. McPherson.

Snerd's door was open. Mr. Oppenheimer looked delighted when he saw Attila. The dog flung himself at his master, but Snerd looked a little apprehensive. Henry leaned over and held his cane across Snerd's shoulder as though it were a sword. I took a deep breath.

"I'm sure, Mr. Snerd," said Henry, "that you told Mr. Oppenheimer who really found the dog?" Mr. Oppenheimer stopped hugging the dog long enough to look at Snerd.

"Mr. Snerd didn't you say...?"

I took the end of Attila's leash and led the dog over to Snerd. He backed up to the wall.

"Attila," I said, and took the dog even closer to Snerd, "do you remember him?" The dog snarled. Snerd gave a little shriek and shouted,

"Take it away, take it away."

"Well?" I said.

"Of course you found it...yes, you found it," said Snerd. His shaky hand reached for his pocket handkerchief and he wiped his face. "I hope...um...Mr. Oppenhiemer; I didn't lead you to believe anything other?"

Me and Henry walked with Mr. Oppenheimer to his car at the front door where he handed me a cheque for a hundred dollars. As the chauffeur drove away, Attila turned round in the back seat. The dog gazed at us till the car was out of sight.

I felt as I did when I saw each of my children leave on the school bus for the first time.

April 24th

I got the cheque from Mr. Oppenheimer copied on the copy machine. I put it under Snerdy Turdy's office door with a note that said, 'Read this and weep.'

April 25th

When I woke this morning I remembered it was one of those boiled egg days. I haven't gotten even with Lorylee yet. I thought about it as I dressed. When I reached for my shoes under the dresser I saw the newspaper parcel and remembered the rat. I picked up the parcel and didn't even wait for Henry. I went straight down to the dining room.

It was twenty to eight when I got to the kitchen. I could see the big steel pan with all the eggs just simmering away.

"Now, Clover!" Lorylee exclaimed as she saw me. "You know this is out of bounds." She looked me up and down. "You know very well you're covered in germs."

"Yes, I know." I said. "It's just I wanted to thank you for marking my special egg the other day."

"Oh, what are friends for, Clover?" she smirked. She turned around to put bread in the big toaster. Quickly, I held a corner of the newspaper and let it unroll, the rat landed right on top of the eggs. It looked hideous. It seemed to increase in size as the water bubbled round it. I crumpled up the newspaper and dropped it in the garbage can near the kitchen doorway. As I passed through the door I called back to her,

"Isn't it time to lift the eggs out, Lorylee?"

"I know, I know, for goodness sake," she snapped. I hadn't quite reached my table when I heard the scream. "I think I'll pass on the eggs this morning," I said to Henry.

May

May 3ʳᵈ

Sometimes delivering these funeral forms can be boring, and then sometimes it can be interesting. Today I went to see Charlie Summersgill. He's just turned ninety, so he might be on his way out soon. I hurried to his room.

"Charlie, can you get off your exercise bike for a minute please?" I asked. "I want to talk about your demise."

"My dewhat?" he asked. He turned off his Tommy Dorsey tape and came to sit beside me on the bed.

"Dying, Charlie, that's what I'm here about."

"Oh, that."

"Yes, now what would you like to happen when you die?"

"Well," he pondered for a moment. "Have you ever been to a waxworks museum, Clover, like Madam Tussaud's?"

"Yes," I told him. "I used to love going to the one in London when I was a youngster."

"Well, what I would like is for them to pour candle grease, or whatever it is, over my dead body and stand me up somewhere forever." I looked at his body; a hundred and ten pounds of sinew and muscle. He looked like he needed ironing.

"I don't know if it works like that, Charlie," I told him. "I don't think they pour that stuff over you. I think they make a cast first."

"I wondered about that," he said peering across at his wardrobe mirror.

"No," I went on, "I don't think the government would put up with that you know...I mean...real bodies...mind you I saw this movie once with Vincent Price. They were murdering people right left and centre and the police couldn't find the bodies. You know why? The bodies were on show at the local waxworks. Then someone recognized their auntie or somebody. At the end it was marvellous because all the wax figures came to life and...." Charlie wasn't listening. He was staring at his picture on the wall. The caption read, 'Senior Weight Lifting Champion.' It was taken twenty-five years ago. Mind you, it didn't seem to help.

"I know Jack the Ripper's standing up somewhere," he grumbled, "I'm just as good as Jack the Ripper." I patted his shoulder and said,

"If you ask me, you're a lot better." He climbed back onto his bike.

"Yes," he said smiling, "Jack the Ripper never cut a nice birthday cake like I did last week when he was ninety." I put the funeral form on his dresser for his son Claude to fill out. Claude comes and takes Charlie to his home every weekend. Charlie does all his odd jobs and cuts his grass. I looked back at Charlie's smiling face, pedalling away happily. I thought to myself, I bet Claude won't be riding a bike when he's ninety.

May 9th

This was a very trying day. I decided to go for a walk on Robson Street. There was a chill in the air, so I wore the fake fur jacket that my daughter Doris brought me last weekend.

"It's Golden Mink, Mother," she told me. "It's synthetic, but doesn't it look nice?"

"Yes, it reminds me of old Toby the cat," I said, "after he'd come home from fighting all night." So off I went round the corner of Honeystone Mansion onto Bute Street. Suddenly, a woman of about fifty appeared out of nowhere. She was wearing jeans and a sweatshirt that said, 'We're all God's Critters.' She was holding a can of red spray paint. The woman pointed the can at my jacket.

"Animal killer," she shouted as she sprayed a large red circle on the front of my fur jacket. I was really angry. I reached out and taking her by surprise, grabbed the can.

"It's flipping fake fur, you fool," I shouted. Then I sprayed a large red dot on her chest. The caption on her sweatshirt now read, 'We're Critters.' I heard a noise and turned to see four of her companions bearing down on me. They were all dressed in the same sweatshirts.

"We're here, Agnes! We're here!" Their cans were poised and ready to spray. I knew I had to get the attention of the few people I saw walking on the other side of the street. It was no good shouting that these people are spraying me with red paint because they think I'm wearing a fur coat. There wasn't time for that.

"Purse snatchers! Purse snatchers!" I shouted. I hadn't even had a purse with me, but it worked. Two young men with tennis racquets under their arms raced over to me. The five spray can carriers stopped dead in their tracks.

"They've got my purse," I shouted. The young men turned to the five women who ran like mad down to the corner. The lights were against them. I stood and watched as the two men wrestled with them. Not knowing which was supposed to be my purse, the two young men confiscated all of theirs. The scuffling and screaming went on for quite a few minutes. One of the store-keepers must have called the police because I could hear sirens in the distance.

Being a peace-loving person I headed quickly back round the corner and into Honeystone Mansion. There was more aggravation to come. The Dolly Sisters were sitting in the foyer facing the door.

"Ooh, look at Clover," said one.

"Ooh, look at Clover," said the other. They both pointed at my chest and together they shouted, "Blood, blood!" They rounded this off with a scream in perfect harmony.

Someone came with a wheelchair. I realized I was very tired and gladly sat down. As the care aide rushed me past the front desk, he called to the receptionist Diane.

"Get Dr. Harrison! Quick!"

Upstairs in my room, Rhodena very carefully removed my jacket.

"Who did this awful thing, Clover?" She was almost in tears. I sank happily onto my bed. Then I thought she should know some of the details of my ordeal.

"There were five of them," I murmured. I remembered then that Doris had given me the coat and now it was likely ruined. "Rhodena, Rhodena," I pleaded, "call my daughter Doris quickly and tell her...tell her..." I forgot what I wanted to say; I was fading off into sleep. I faintly heard Rhodena.

"Yes, yes, yes," she said as she stroked my hand. The ghastly events of the day were slipping away when I heard the voice of Dr. Harrison. Rhodena jumped up from the bed and the doctor sat down.

"I've just been looking at your fur jacket, Clover," he told me.

"Yes," I said, "isn't it terrible what one human being will do to another?"

He interrupted me, "I hope you realize, Clover, that the staff considered sending you to St. Paul's Hospital to have a bullet removed." Drowsiness was taking over and I barely heard the rest of what he was saying. He seemed to be questioning why I had ruined his golf game because of choosing to do some painting in a fur jacket.

May 12th

Snerd came to my room today. He had my fur coat over his arm; it was fresh from the cleaners. He held it up.

"Fifty-two dollars this cost!" He shook the jacket as though it was a live dog that had just wet his carpet. "Fifty-two dollars!" he went on, his skinny frame dithering. "Oh, I fought with administration about it, don't think I didn't." He shook the coat again. "But no, they wouldn't listen." He threw the jacket on the bed.

"Fifty-two dollars, eh?" I said. "That's funny, because it only cost twelve dollars when my daughter bought it at the Salvation Army thrift store." Snerd wiped some dribble from the corner of his mouth.

"You're a cost clerk's living nightmare," he said as he opened the door.

"Thanks," I said, "I'll let everyone know that you dream about me...dream lover," I said, blowing him a kiss.

May 19th

I called in on Monster again today. He's still not talking, but I never give up hope.

"Your walls are bare," I pointed out to him. "You need some pictures. I could make this place look like home." He stared at me. "I have lots of pictures. I've got a nice one of the Queen signing the Magna Charter of Rights. I've a calendar from last year. It has pictures of the best looking firemen in Vancouver, and I also have some nice kitten pictures." Then I remembered something. Ms. McPherson had sent round a memo saying, 'Please do not stick things on the walls. We want a homelike atmosphere at Honeystone Mansion.'

"Hang on," I told him. I realized the memo was right, sticky tape looks tacky. "I think I know where I can get a hammer and some nails. I'll be back."

May 20th

Fortunately, I have made it my business to know when Dick, the maintenance man, is off duty, and this is his day off. I also know where he keeps his wagon. I found a hammer, but only one nail; it was a nice big one though. It would do to make the holes for all the pictures I intend to put on Monster's wall. I went back to Monster's room. He was sitting on the side of his bed.

"Hi," I said. "I've come to make a row of holes where I think the pictures should go." He gazed right through me. "I'll get more nails to fit the holes later."

I locked the door because I hate being interrupted while I'm creating. I hammered about eleven holes in a row using the one six-inch nail. The holes were as high as my arm could reach. I kept stopping and chatting to Monster to give my blood a chance to circulate back through my arms. Each time I hammered I was sure I could hear things falling on the other side of the wall. Nettie Spooner lives next door to Monster. It's probably the echo of me banging, I thought to myself. Monster sat quietly watching me. "We'll need something really special for the middle hole," I told him.

As I was leaving, I looked back at the wall. I had to admit, it looked as though someone with a nervous disorder had peppered the wall with a machine gun.

"Soon," I told him, "I'll get some nails and put the pictures up. If you like them I'll put holes in the other wall too," but Monster shook his head from side to side. I don't think he wanted me to go.

May 22nd

We have a discussion group on Monday afternoons. I hear some idiotic conversations there. The Dolly Sisters love discussions. They repeat everything each other says. It's uncanny the way they do everything the same. They even pee exactly the same length of time; I know–I've timed them.

Today Nettie Spooner, Monster's neighbour, who thinks she's an authority on the occult, said she believes Honeystone Mansion is haunted.

"Tell us why you think that," said Susan the activity aide, while she tried to hide a yawn.

"Well," Nettie went on, "you know my beautiful fan collection?"

"Yes, Nettie, you've got them all over your wall," said Susan.

"Well, yesterday the whole row of them fell down," she said.

"One–after the other–after the other." She looked around and went on in a hoarse whisper. "As each one fell, I heard a strange hollow bang. Yes, the spirits were calling me."

I couldn't help saying, "It's a pity you can't get the spirits to come and dust your fans once in a while."

"Poltergeist," said one of the Dolly Sisters.

"Poltergeist," said the other.

"Yes," I agreed, "you could be right. You two had better watch that collection of Toby jugs you've got." That made their little curls dance!

May 23rd

I bought a pound of nails today from the hardware store around the corner. I needed big ones to fit the holes I'd made in Monster's wall. I also found the special picture I needed for the middle spot. It was in the quiet room where nobody goes because it's so dark and depressing. It was a picture of an old lady sitting in a chair. It was quite light for its size. None of the staff saw me take it up to the fourth floor. I showed it to Monster and he loved it; he held it to his stomach and crooned. I had to pry it out of his hands to put it on the wall. Some of the pictures I brought him were torn out of old calendars. I just made holes in them and slipped them over the nails. The room looked really nice. I left Monster staring at the old lady on the wall.

May 26th

At breakfast this morning I heard a voice over the loud-speaker that sounded like the cost clerk, Snerdy Turdy. He was saying, "Will whoever took the picture of <u>Whistler's Mother</u>, please return it? No questions will be asked."

"They're always losing stuff," I said to Henry.

May 27th

The woman I admire most in the world, except of course for the Queen, is the pigeon lady. I watch her often at the little green area close by. It's known as Nelson Park. She arrives each day with a shopping cart full of food for the birds. She looks like any other ordinary person until she steps onto the grass. Swirling clouds of pigeons come from all around. Hundreds of them land at her feet, some hover in the air around her shoulders. They make nice little cooing noises as she throws seed out for them.

Me and Henry were sitting on one of the benches watching her today. I was enthralled; Henry nodded off to sleep. He woke with a start when a few 'anti-pigeon' people came along. They clapped their hands and shouted to frighten the birds away.

"Get away, you jealous sods," the pigeon lady shouted at them. The birds fluttered into the air just above the ground, then landed even closer to her. Her voice didn't seem to bother the birds at all. "Ignorant people like you can learn a lot from these birds."

"Yes," one of them shouted back, "like how to shit over everything."

"Piss off, you miserable bastards," she retaliated. I looked at Henry.

"She is a very special person," I told him.

"Personally, I think she's a bad-mouthed crazy woman," said Henry.

"You don't understand, Henry," I told him. "This woman has a God-given gift and the birds know it."

"Clover! There's a sign right beside her. Look. It says, 'Don't feed the pigeons.'"

"Oh Henry, Henry, Henry," I said. "This woman walks to a different drummer than you and I."

"Well, right now," said Henry, "she's walking in a lot of pigeon shit. Let's go home for lunch." As we got up I watched the pigeon lady shake the last few seeds onto the ground and wheel her cart away. The birds hung around pecking for a while, then they flew off. The whole park seemed empty and quiet. As we walked home to Honeystone Mansion I thought about her. Why couldn't I be like her and have birds coming at my command? I decided to at least give it a try.

May 28th

I went round the tables at lunch today after most people had eaten. We had cheesecake for dessert. I got lots of nice big pieces from the cart marked 'Staff Only.' I hovered beside the table always occupied by the Dolly Sisters hoping to get their leftover cheesecake. Arthur Proctor beat me to it.

"You're not going to spoil your gorgeous figures with this stuff, are you?" he asked leering at them. They both giggled.

"You are awful, Arthur," one of them said.

"Yes, you're awful!" said the other.

"And you're awful pretty," he purred, as he scooped their two pieces of cheesecake into a dirty cotton handkerchief. I gave him a thump as I passed by and left him picking up bits of cake from the floor.

I didn't say anything to Henry as I went out alone to the park. Miracles only seem to happen when you're on your own. I'm sure Joan of Arc wouldn't have had that vision, or whatever it was she had, if she'd had her boyfriend with her at the time. When I got to the park, I scattered the cheesecake in a circle around me and waited. A couple of stray pigeons flew low. I pointed at the crumbled pieces of cheesecake on the ground.

"Come and get it," I shouted. The birds wheeled around as though looking for someone. Then, sure enough, there she was. The pigeon lady arrived and put one foot on the grass. Suddenly the air was full of birds.

"Terrific! Terrific!" I shouted. "Come on, come on," I beckoned to her.

"What do you think you're doing?" she barked. "What the Hell are you doing on my turf?" The birds were circling over her head.

"I want the birds to come to me like they do for you," I said.

"Go get your own bloody birds," she replied.

"You've got them all," I told her.

"Well, that's too bloody bad, isn't it?" she shouted. I began to feel a bit rattled.

"You can't stand competition, that's what the problem is," I said. She took a couple of steps toward me.

"Move it. Go on, move it!" She didn't scare me. Well, not much...

"Make me." I made sure I stayed inside my circle of cheesecake. She came closer. Now we were both standing under a cloud of birds. It felt great. I looked up. The sky was full of hovering pigeons. Here I was in this little place called Nelson Park and I couldn't help shouting those immortal words of Shakespeare. "'And they shall hold their womanhood cheap who were not here today on Nelson Field.'"

"You're a raving bloody idiot," she said as I tried to think of the next few lines. I was about to go on when a police car came round the corner. The car stopped on the edge of the park. A policeman came over.

"What's all this?" He was pointing to the cheesecake. The birds were still hovering but in a wider and higher circle. "Pick all this garbage up, or else." He took out a notebook.

"It's not garbage," I told him. "It's cheesecake, for the birds." To prove my point I started to holler at the sky. "Come on, come on!" The policeman tapped his notebook with his pencil then pointed at the sign close by.

"You've got two misdemeanours here. A, you're littering, and B, you're feeding the pigeons." The pigeon woman stood smirking with her hands on her hips. The policeman's partner was now heading toward us. Just as he got a few yards onto the grass a pigeon dropped a big blob of white goo down the side of his face.

"Aw...shit." This seemed to be a signal for all the birds to do just that. The first policeman had started writing out a ticket when a big white splatter fell in the middle of his book. He slammed it shut and the book seemed to spit from all sides. He waved forcefully at the birds. His partner turned back to the car. He was bent over, holding his hands on his head as though defending himself from heavy rain. Back at the car he shouted to his partner.

"Aw, shit! Look at the car! Steve...Come on, look at the pissing car." Steve looked at the car, hesitated a second then ran. His partner had already started the engine.

I was left with the birds and the pigeon woman. She ignored me and scattered her birdseed to one side of me. I stood in my circle of cake watching her. The pigeons had descended to the ground all around her.

I began to wish I had eaten the cheesecake myself, when suddenly I heard a terrible shrieking. Half a dozen seagulls landed in front of me. They saw the cheesecake and started a frenzy of squealing and squalling. They were joined by a few more. Like hungry vultures they pounced on my cake and devoured it. The pigeons looked nervous. They began to scatter. The pigeon woman shook her arms at my seagulls. They ignored her. The few pigeons that remained were now high above us on the telephone wires.

"Get out to sea where you belong, you bloody rotten scavengers," she screamed.

"They're enjoying my cheesecake if you don't mind," I told her.

"Stupid idiot...feeding birds cheesecake," she snapped. I took a step in her direction. I was surprised when the seagulls followed me. I walked toward her again. She backed away to the edge of the park. I looked down at my band of seagulls.

"Get her!" I shouted. There must have been something in the tone of my voice because they rose into the air and moved toward her. She fled. Her cart rattled along as she made her way toward Davie Street.

You're a born leader, Clover, I said to myself. I turned to pay homage to my stalwart band of seagulls. But they were gone.

When I got back to Honeystone Mansion, Henry was waiting for me in the foyer.

"Is it snowing?" he asked. "You're covered in white blotches."

I looked down at myself and laughed.

"Oh, no. They're battle scars," I told him.

June

June 3ʳᵈ

Today I felt in the mood for a challenge. I decided to ask Monster what kind of funeral he'd like. I thought maybe I could suggest a few things and he could nod when I hit the right one. He was sitting on the side of his bed staring at the picture of the old lady I had put on the wall. I sat beside him.

"I'd like to help you to fill out this form." I waved the papers in front of his face. This caught his attention and he looked at me. I plunged right in and told him about various types of funerals. I explained what cremation was all about. He looked a bit taken aback when I said,

"You get put in a box and then into an oven. They do give your relatives some of your ashes though, in a very nice urn."

He didn't seem impressed; it was as though he had forgotten everything about dying and living.

I discussed common-or-garden burials. "They lower you in a wooden box into a hole in the ground," I told him. He just stared sadly at me. In an attempt to lighten up the conversation, I said, "Of course, if you're a vampire they put a stake through your heart." He didn't smile.

I talked for a while on mausoleums; I explained to him that I had once read a beautiful brochure on the subject. "It told," I said, "how the worms can't eat you because you're airtight in this big marble wall unit." He was looking very scared when I'd finished. Then I realized I hadn't told him that you had to die before any of these things could happen. Before I could explain it all from scratch, there was a knock at the door.

"Listen," I said, "stop shaking. I'll explain it all again later." I went and opened the door and there was Snerdy Turdy.

"If I were you," I pointed out to him, "I wouldn't bother Monster just now. He's a bit upset."

"If you don't mind, I have important business here." Snerd pushed past me into the room. He turned and gave me a little shove, which sent me tottering through the door. He then slammed the door in my face. I waited a while in the hall. As I expected, Monster's door flew open in a couple of minutes. Snerd came staggering out. He had the picture of the old lady under one arm. With his other hand he was holding his nose. I bobbed quickly into the room next door, Nettie Spooner's room. I've discovered in my life that things don't always work out as they should. It was just a portrait of old lady, after all. Anyone would think it was a picture of Snerd's own mother.

Come to think of it, she did look pretty fed up!

June 6th

Henry's gone into hospital for a few days; more stuff to do with his leg.

Maisey asked me where Henry was. "He's gone to the university for tests," I told her.

She said, "Don't worry, he'll do well. He's very intelligent."

Sometimes I wonder about this woman.

June 12th

I'm still missing Henry a bit. I know he would have enjoyed sharing this evening. I'd been at The Pig and Whistle Pub and I was feeling quite mellow about life as I returned to Honeystone, about eleven thirty. Quite often, as I pass the rhododendrons that grow around the front door, I see skunks. Being nocturnal, skunks like the night. I enjoy seeing them and I have the feeling that some of them have been here for years. Honeystone's gardener, old Ernie, says, "I just work around the little critters. They don't bother me and I don't bother them."

I have a favourite one. I call her Mrs. Fanackapan. I'm sure it's a she because earlier this year I saw her with some little ones. Tonight I heard rustling among the bushes and there she was. She's getting heavier and slower in her old age, like me. She waddled out in front of me snuffling at the ground. I caught up to her and we walked the curved path leading to the door together.

"Let me see what I've got for you tonight," I said. I always have bits of food in my handbag. I dropped some pieces of dried apple in front of her. She stopped to nibble.

"You know, Mrs. Fanackapan, you and me have seen better days." I knew she was listening as she munched.

"We're both outcasts of society," I told her. She finished the apple and we moved on. "Yes, we're two of a kind." She stopped to inspect some orange peel just as the automatic front door flew open. Clive, the night care aide, peered out.

"Clover, is that you?" he called. "Get in here. You're the last one in as usual."

"I'm just talking to a friend," I told him.

"Who are you talking too? You know I'll be in trouble if you're not in soon, Clover," he said. "I have to lock this door at midnight, that's the rule."

"I'm conversing with my friend, if you don't mind," I told him again.

57

"For God sakes," he said, "get in here and bring your friend with you."

"Well," I looked down at Mrs. Fanackapan, "you heard the man."

I walked slowly through the automatic door sprinkling bits of apple on the way and we both strolled inside. The door closed behind us. Clive and the night nurse Tanya were sitting behind the reception desk. They both glanced over. I knew that Clive had done some ballet dancing in his life, but I never saw him move so fast. He vaulted over the desk and dived for the elevator. Tanya screamed. Poor Mrs. Fanackapan started twisting round and round as though chasing her tail.

"Get out! Get out!" Tanya yelled from a top the swivel chair she was tottering on.

"If my friend's going, then I'm going," I told them. I stepped toward the door, it automatically opened and Mrs. Fanackapan fled. I was aware of a burning in my nostrils.

Clive was still standing by the elevator; his back a ramrod against the doors, his arms outstretched. As the doors opened he almost fell backwards.

"Clover," he shouted, as he steadied himself, "don't move... just wait there. When I've gone, get the next elevator. I'll be waiting for you on four."

Tanya was nowhere in sight. I did as Clive told me. I got off on my floor. Clive was waiting. He had on a mask and an apron. He motioned me into the big main bathroom. Polly, the other care aide, was running a bath.

"Quick! Quick! Take all your clothes off," she said while holding her nose with one hand and trying the temperature of the water with the other.

"We have to burn them," said Clive, talking through his mask. I was too tired to argue.

Soon I lay soaking in the bath. Clive came back and sat on a small stool at the other side of the plastic curtain.

"I've thrown all your clothes in the incinerator, Clover," he told me. I was very tired and upset.

"You and Tanya frightened Mrs. Fanackapan," I explained. "It wasn't her fault."

"I know, Clover, but you do the craziest things." He reached his arm around the curtain and massaged my back. "I like skunks too, Clover," he said, "I just think they're darling little things." I told him I didn't care about the sweater and the underwear, but I did like the dress. He handed me two nice big towels even though the rule says only one. He got me a chair and hunched down beside me. "You know, Clover, when you lose anything here, Mr. Snerd has to reimburse you for it." I suddenly felt wide awake.

"Clive," I said, "get me the latest Sears Catalogue. I saw one at the nursing station." Clive brought it to me.

"Look," I showed him, "you see that nice little blue dress on the front page? That's what I want." Clive laughed.

"It's eighty-nine dollars! I can just see Snerd's face when we tell him!" he said. We smiled at each other. He did a clever ballet leap to the door as Polly came in with my nightdress and led me off to bed.

June 13th

I remember having a dream last night about Snerdy Turdy. He was foaming at the mouth and in some sort of cage. When I came to visit him I was carrying a skunk.

It was wearing a blue dress.

June 16th

I was so glad to see Henry when he arrived back today. They had made him a nicer artificial leg at the university hospital. He looked great and was just in time to go on our bus trip. All the fourth floor residents were going to the community college.

Some of us were just touring the building and a few of us had booked a hairdressing session. We were told that the students taking the hairdressing course were looking forward to practicing on us. I have my granddaughter's wedding coming up tomorrow, so I wanted to look good.

Arthur Proctor and Henry were taken off to a different part of the salon for their appointments. A friendly bunch of students gathered round us women and asked how we would like our hair done. The Dolly Sisters showed the students a picture of Shirley Temple doing a tap dance. A few of the students were Asian. They smiled and nodded. They thought it was a granddaughter or something. Then one of them said, pointing to Shirley's hair,

"Ah, spirals." As far as I'm concerned, both of the sisters are loop-the-loop, so their hair might as well be the same.

I sat in one of the comfortable hairdressing chairs and listened to the hum of conversation. I was almost dozing off when a tall, pale-faced young woman came over to me. Her jet-black hair stood on end. It had been separated into about twenty clumps and each rigid clump ended with a sharp purple tip.

"So...how would you like your hair?" she asked as she fluffed my hair with both her hands.

"Well," I said, "I was thinking of...maybe just little curls all round...you know?"

"Yuck," she put her finger into her mouth and pretended to be sick. "Look," she said with a shrug, "I'll tell one of the others what you want. Some of the students will do anything." She pretended to be sick again. I watched her walk away and a little later a young Asian girl came over.

"How you like?" she pointed to my hair. "How you like?"

"Didn't she tell you?" I pointed to the girl with the purple tips who was now at the other end of the room.

"You mean her?" she pointed toward the same girl. "Wait one moment, I go ask how." She came back in a short while, a smile on her face. She led me to the sink and washed my hair. Back at her workstation, I sat comfortably feeling pampered and happy.

I closed my eyes. I was aware of soothing hands working on my hair. I vaguely remember another trip to the sink. Gentle fingers stroked my hair as I fell asleep.

When I opened my eyes, the mirror was right in front of me. I looked at the reflection. A perfect stranger looked back. She had gray spikes all over her head. The young Asian girl smiled over my shoulder as she put blobs of purple wax over the end of each spike. I spoke, and realized the person in the mirror was me.

"Did I happen to tell you," I asked the girl, "that I'm going to my granddaughter's wedding tomorrow?" I was trying to remain calm. I looked closer into the mirror. The young student nodded and smiled proudly at me. Suddenly, I couldn't help laughing.

"You pleased? I can tell you pleased." She stood back and beckoned all the students around. "Look," she said, pointing at me. "First time I do this." They crowded round all smiling at me in the mirror. Then someone pushed through the small crowd and, bending, put her face next to mine. It was the tall, purple-tip girl. We looked at each other's reflections.

"Way to go, Grandma!" she said.

"Yes, but is it the way to go to my granddaughter's wedding?" I asked.

"It sure is," she answered.

Everyone from Honeystone was waiting for me outside in the hall. I thought the laughing would never subside. We stood for quite a while discussing our hair-do's. Henry had a really smart crew cut.

"It takes me back to the army days," he said. "They wouldn't have me, but at least now I've got the hair cut." Arthur Proctor swaggered around. He looked at his reflection in the window of the salon.

"This," he told us, "is what all the smart young people are wearing now. Or so they tell me." His hair looked as though someone had taken a miniature lawn mower and ran it down the middle of his thick untidy hair. "Whaderya think?" he asked me.

"Well," I answered, "let's think of it as just a very wide part." The Dolly Sisters were shaking their spiral hair-do's around, hoping someone would notice. Everybody did because they got tangled up in each other's spiral curls. I pulled them apart.

"Listen," I announced, "we all look so good let's not call the bus. Let's walk home."

We passed a lot of smiling faces on the way. We only caused one minor traffic accident when a couple of cars stopped. One driver asked where the rest of the parade was. The driver behind him kept honking his horn and frowning at us as he moved forward without looking, and bumped into the back of a van. We caught up to him just as the van driver came round to assess the damage. The driver was now scowling at us. I called over to him.

"Envy does terrible things, doesn't it?" I didn't catch his answer.

Back at Honeystone we caused a bit of stir in the dining room at suppertime.

Ms. McPherson did her usual rounds of the dining room tables. She usually glides by after smiling once at each table. She stopped at my table.

"Did we fall into something purple, Clover?" she asked with a false dazed look on her face. I looked up and smiled sweetly.

"Yes, we did," I replied, "I don't know about you, but someone held me by the ankles, and dipped me into some grape juice. It was more fun than I ever get around here."

Henry said, without looking up from his soup. "You've got really nice ankles, Clover."

Ms. McPherson gave a snort of disgust and moved on. That night I slept sitting up in my armchair. I didn't want to ruin my hair-do.

June 17th

My daughter-in-law Gerty called me this morning.

"Did you have your hair done then, Mother?" she asked.

"Yes, of course I've had my hair done," I told her, "I wouldn't come to Gillian's wedding without having my hair done, would I?" There were a few seconds of silence.

"Does it look nice?" Gerty asked.

"Well...It's different," I said.

"Oh, you tried something new?"

"Yes," I said, "I'm wearing it up."

"Good, that sounds sophisticated." I distinctly hear a loud sniff. I looked at my reflection in the mirror as I spoke to her.

"Sometimes," I pointed out, "I think we should be willing to take chances...to dare to be different."

"Oh, have you got rid of the gray, then?"

"Some," I replied.

"I'm sure you'll look lovely, Mother. Now, what are you wearing?" She was practically purring.

"I'm wearing," I said, "the dress that's on the front cover of the Sears June catalogue...it was a gift from Mr. Snerd the cost clerk."

"That's funny, Mother," she said, "I always got the feeling that Mr. Snerd didn't like you very much."

"Well," I told her, "I can be quite irresistible when I want to be, you know." There was a pause.

"If you say so, Mother. Anyway, Sandy will come and pick you and Henry up," she said. "See you later."

Henry looked so handsome in his dark blue suit. He really liked my blue dress. It came nearly to my ankles and had a bolero jacket that came to my waist. I wore the necklace that Sandy bought me for Christmas. It was a chain with a great big blue stone in the middle. He told me it was the necklace from the Titanic. He'd seen it in the movie and apparently thought the necklace would be perfect for me. Sandy arrived about eleven o'clock. He usually rushes in with a hug, and then tells me all his latest news. This time he stopped in the doorway.

"And I thought my sister's wedding would be boring!" He gave us both a hug. "And look at you, big guy," he said to Henry. Sandy had a bit of trouble concentrating on his driving on the way to the church. He kept looking at me in the rear view mirror and laughing.

"I guess it's going to be a great day for taking photos, Grandma," he said.

Sandy proudly led me and Henry down the aisle of the church to the front pew. I could feel the stares. I could hear the "oohs" and the "aahs." By now, me and Henry were used to all this. We finally reached the first pew. As we brushed past Gerty to get to the other side of her, she hissed at me,

"Did you purposely set out to steal the limelight from my Gillian?" Henry gave my hand a squeeze. Gerty got so agitated someone had to run and get her a tranquilizer.

Soon the wedding music started. Gillian came down the aisle looking lovely on my son Fred's arm. Almost at the altar, she turned toward me and her mother. I waved to her. She hesitated for a second. Gerty was crying. Then Fred looked my way. He stopped dead. Gillian, who was now giggling, dragged her father the last few feet to the altar.

Later at the photo studio, Gerty insisted the photographer put tall people in front of me. Fortunately, Sandy took pictures at the reception and made sure I was in all of them. Sandy introduced me to Larry, the groom. I hadn't met him before; he had been away a lot working on an oilrig. Larry was pale and nervous. He shook my hand very gently.

"You're Gillian's grandma." I smiled, hoping for some further input. He said, "I happen to know Gillian thinks you're... funny and fantastic, that's the way she puts it. You're from the... err...institution aren't you?" he asked.

"Yes," I answered. "They had me put away."

"I see." He looked around for help. I could see that he found this much scarier than working on an oilrig. He grinned, not knowing what else to say. I didn't help; I think young people should be encouraged to practice the art of conversation. "They told me you were doing strange things." As he looked at my hair he said, "So...you're out on...parole? I mean..."

"Yes, they've let me out for good behaviour," I told him. "And I'd just like to give you a word of warning," I pointed my finger at him. "You know this could happen to you."

"What?"

"You could be put away like me," I said. He looked over his shoulder quite scared.

"Go on," he said.

"Well, just don't start forgetting things, or losing your socks or else..." I glanced at Gerty who was on her way over to us. "They'll put you away," I whispered. He looked visibly shaken as Gerty grabbed his arm and whipped him away to cut the cake. I couldn't help thinking that the way he was shaking, I wouldn't have put a knife in his hand.

To make things worse, or better, whichever way you looked at it, Sandy secretly got me to bob up behind Larry and Gillian just as they bent to cut the wedding cake. The crowd laughed. The photo might give the happy couple a smile later on. Sandy also took a picture of me in the centre of the four bridesmaids. They didn't mind a bit! Then Sandy gave me and Henry a bottle of champagne and he took a picture of us pouring it into Gerty's 'non-alcoholic' fruit punch.

Me and Henry danced several times on the tiny dance floor. His artificial leg seemed to make the tango a bit jerkier, but that was fine. We laughed as my wax purple tips began to melt under the hot lights. Around eleven we whispered to Sandy that we were both feeling tired and that it was time to go. Sandy called us a taxi and handed Henry another bottle of champagne. Sandy gave me a kiss and said, "You sure made my day, Grandma."

Me and Henry had one last nightcap in his room when we got back.

"Well," said Henry, "I gotta get this old leg off and get to bed."

"Don't worry, I'll help," I offered. There was a lot more laughing when I realized I was trying to pull off the wrong leg. We collapsed on Henry's bed and both fell asleep.

June 21ˢᵗ

I got back to my forms today. I called on the Dolly Sisters. They were changing the water in their small, round, goldfish bowl. One of them was setting up the little figures at the bottom.

I watched as she placed a small treasure chest in the bowl and on top of the chest she set a reclining bosomy mermaid. She then put in a lobster trap. A lobster's claw stuck out between the slats. Then she dropped in a piece of red sponge, which stayed on the bottom because the leg of a G. I. Joe action figure had been rammed through the middle of it. The last thing she put into the crowded bowl was a miniature wooden totem pole. The pole was wedged into a piece of modelling clay.

While she was doing this, the other sister was nodding and smiling. She was also holding an open plastic denture dish, about four inches square, and it contained their two small gold-fish called Bobby and Berty. Both were flopping around in the dish. They looked like two little children trying to see what was over a brick wall. The fish, I could see, were intent on making a getaway.

I reached over and flipped the lid closed. The first sister took this as a sign to speed up. She grabbed a small teapot and ran to the washroom for water. Back and forth she ran. Each time she reached the fish tank she gave a frightened look at the denture dish, as though she expected little shrieks from Bobby and Berty. I knew this would take time.

I made myself comfortable on one of their comfy wicker chairs. I didn't dare talk about funerals while one of the twins was holding the denture dish. I let the first sister do about five trips to the washroom with the teapot. Then I got impatient. I grabbed the denture dish and tipped it into the fishbowl. Bobby and Berty gasped a bit because they were just barely covered with water. Both sisters started twittering.

The twin with the teapot really sped up. She was like a mechanical toy, darting back and forth to the washroom getting water. The other twin now joined the water brigade. She used the denture dish as a container. Somehow they managed not to collide as they ran. I waited till the bowl was two thirds full. I couldn't stand any more.

"Have you two made any funeral arrangements?" I asked. They stopped in their tracks.

"Yes. We have our own little plot," said one.

"With a lovely view," said the other.

"Oh, don't forget your glasses then," I suggested.

"We'll be buried together," said one.

"Yes, together," said the other.

"Do you mean in the same box?" I asked.

"Oh, we never thought of that," said one.

"No, we hadn't thought of that," said the other.

"Let's think about it now," I suggested. They smiled and nodded at each other. "You'll have to get together on the date, of course." They looked at me in bewilderment. This is their usual expression. "Well, you can't have one waiting in the box for the other," I pointed out. "These things have to be well planned." Boy do these two need help, I thought.

"Oh, we do everything together," one of the sisters murmured.

"Everything," agreed the other.

I wrote all the stuff they had just said in the empty space for comments on the bottom of the form.

"Here," I told them, "fill out the rest of it. Let me know when you're feeling sick, this is one funeral I don't want to miss."

"Oh, you must be there, Clover," said one.

"Oh, you must," said the other.

I left them pondering which funeral home they should write in the space on the form. I tried to visualize the coffin. They're both four foot eight inches tall. That would make the coffin almost square. Then I had a bright idea...they could use one funeral plot by having the coffin dropped in the hole on its end. I'm all for saving money whenever possible. I'll explain that to them later.

June 25th

Gerty sent me one of the wedding photos today. It was a group picture. I had trouble finding myself then I realized she'd had the photographer black out my hair. "This amounts to censorship," I told Henry. He agreed.

Thank goodness young Sandy took some real photos.

June 27th

I brushed crumbs off the top of my funeral forms today. I also discovered a tea stain which went through four layers, so I threw them out. I have only ten forms left. I'll give them to the ones who are likely to go first. Me and Henry will make it to a hundred. We can wait. I decided to give a funeral form to the family of my roommate Maisey. I think I should tell them that the way she keeps falling they could leave a coffin by the side of her bed. Sooner or later she'll fall in. I could never be heartless like that, of course, so I'll just tell them to fill out the form because her days are numbered.

I also called in to see Arthur Proctor. I walked through his ever-open door. I am always amazed at the speed of this man. He leapt off his bed, grabbed me round the waist and with his right foot slammed the door shut. I'm told he was an expert soccer player in his day.

"It's just you and me, my little chickadee," he muttered. I slapped him with the bundle of funeral forms. Now the top one had spit on it. Arthur splutters a bit when he gets emotional.

"I'll have you know," I told him, "I'm here on very serious business."

"Good, that's what I'm here for," he said puckering his lips. "Serious business." I gave him a push then and threw the spit stained form on his bed.

"I'm here to discuss your demise," I informed him. He picked up the form.

"Here, what d'yer mean? You know something I don't know?" He held the form up to his face and screwed up his little blue eyes. "Did the doctor tell you something? Come on...come on...tell me." I went to the doorway and in my best Mae West voice said,

"Sorry, kid, but all I know is...we've all gotta go."

"She's a poet too," he yelled in his Cary Grant voice. He made a final lunge at me, but I made for the door and struggled with the knob. "You can't fight it, Clover, so don't pretend. You're mine, all m...."

I got the door open, gave him a quick kick in the shins then slammed the door in his face.

June 28th

I noticed the Dolly Sisters were each wearing one black silk stocking today. They wore the stocking tied round their left arms just above the elbow. They do such weird things, but they always have a reason. I asked them about it as me and Henry walked with them to the elevator.

"So, what's with the black stockings round your arms?" I asked.

"We're in mourning, Clover."

"Yes, in mourning."

"Anyone I know?" I asked.

"Bobby."

"And Berty," they each said. The names rang a bell with me. I tried to remember but couldn't.

"Are there more twins in your family then?" Henry asked.

He's always polite and sympathetic with these two dotty women.

"No," said one.

"No," said the other. I tried to be patient. I knew they wanted to keep our attention. They love what they call meaningful conversation.

"We mean Bobby."

"And Berty."

Then together they said, "Our goldfishes."

"Well, you know," I couldn't help saying, "if I was sharing a bowl with a crab pot, a GI Joe, and a mermaid, I think I'd get sick too. By the way," I said, looking down at their legs, "did you know your other stockings are at half mast?" They both looked down with a yelp. "Gotcha," I said.

You have to try and cheer people up if you can.

June 30ᵗʰ

My youngest son, Fred, and his wife Gerty came to see me today. He doesn't look anything like fifty. Gerty does, and she's forty-two. I realized I hadn't done my own funeral form, so I asked Fred what he would do if I died.

"Well, Mother," he said, "I'll cry a bit."

"No, no, I know that," I said. "I mean the funeral arrangements?"

"Well," he answered, "we've got you booked in at the Serenity Funeral Parlour on Marine Drive."

Gerty smiled sweetly as she pointed out, "It's got lovely plush carpets and embossed wallpaper. It's surrounded by lovely gardens."

They made it sound as though I was going to Club Med.

July

July 1st

This evening, me and Henry were sitting on his bed. I had helped him off with his new leg. He has a very simple method of dealing with his artificial leg. At night he lifts his good left leg out of his pants, then the pants and the false leg come off together. In the morning he slips his good leg into the pants and his right stump goes into the hollow top of the artificial leg, which is still inside the right leg of his pants. The artificial leg is held on tight by a Velcro strap. This strap is fastened to a leather holster which he slips over his right shoulder.

It was quite romantic really. There we were reclining on Henry's bed, him in his undershorts and me in my dressing gown, drinking hot chocolate and eating ginger snaps. Henry has a wonderful sense of humour. I asked him where he lost his leg. He said,

"Oh, I didn't lose it; I know exactly where I left it." He went on. "It got cut off by a train when I was young. I left the prairies, you see, with lots of other farmhands. There was no work, so we all decided to ride the rails out here to the west coast. The RCMP was given instructions by the government to stop us any way they could. I guess they thought there were enough people out west. Anyway, there was a bit of a demonstration on the station platform and the Mounties used tear gas. I tried to scramble out of the way, but I fell on the track just as the train moved."

"I'm glad I found the rest of you," I told him. He put his hands behind his head. He was in a reminiscent mood.

"Did I tell you, Clover, I went back to the prairies? I even rode horses again. I'd swing the old wooden leg over the horse's back." He laughed. "Someone had to bend it though and get it in the stirrup. The leg I have now is a big improvement, I can tell you."

I asked him if that was when he wore the Stetson I had seen in his wardrobe? "You bet," he said. "You know, Clover...I often have a hankering to ride a horse just one more time." I hugged him.

"I've got a marvellous idea," I told him. "I'll see you tomorrow."

I left him gazing at the ceiling. It was ten after eleven when I got to my room. I phoned my son Fred. I could tell straight away that I'd woken him up. I could hear Gerty in the background.

"Is that your mother again? Give that phone to me." I could hear some muffled grunting going on. Gerty must have won the battle because I heard her bellow into the phone. "Mother, couldn't this wait? What is it this time?"

"I want you to be here early in the morning," I told her.

"We're not signing you out, Mother, so don't ask us..."

"Shut up and listen," I said. "I want you to take me and Henry to some riding stables in Langley..."

Astonished she said, "Mother, you're not getting on a horse."

I could hear Fred in the background, "What, what, she's betting on a horse?"

"No, she's getting on one," said Gerty. As it happened I had no intention of getting on a horse but she got my back up.

"What I do is my business. Be here at six in the morning," I told her and hung up.

July 2nd

They didn't come, but they sent my grandson Sandy. That was fine; being eighteen he loves any excuse to get his hands on the car. Sandy parked in the alley just below my window and honked the horn. A few bad-tempered people shouted down at him. They were complaining about the noise at six o'clock on Sunday morning. Some people have nothing better to do than lie in bed. I hurried to Henry's room down the hall.

"Quick," I said. "Get your leg on and grab your Stetson. We're going out."

Sandy got us to Langley in no time. There was hardly any traffic on the road. Me and Henry hung on to each other; we had to, Sandy kept changing from one empty lane to another. As he swooped back and forth he told us he was just practicing for rush hour traffic.

"I brought the camera along, Grandma," he told me, "I want to use the film up. I can't wait to see the wedding pictures, can you?" We all laughed.

"I already saw the studio photo," I told him, "they blocked out my purple tips!"

"Don't worry, Grandma," he said, "I'll get the negative. The girl at the photo shop is sweet on me...well she will be when I ask her out." Such confidence is wonderful, I thought to myself.

Henry was enjoying the ride but it was time to fill him in on things.

"Henry," I said, "I haven't told you where we're going and why I made you bring your Stetson."

"That's okay," he told me, "I'm with you and Sandy, that's enough for me." I explained how I had phoned the riding stable and how they had told me they get started as soon as the sun comes up. Henry waved his hat in the air and hugged me. I have to admit I was excited too.

When we got there the horses looked so big. A group of people were already mounted and ready to go. Henry walked up to one of the horses waiting for a rider. He stroked its nose and led it to a young man who seemed to be running the show. The young man held the reins and they were both surprised when I stepped forward.

"Henry, I just want a picture on a horse. I want to annoy Gerty." The young man took my arm and pulled me gently to the horse.

"Um...don't you have a smaller thinner one?" I asked. The young man looked at me as though I had insulted his mother.

"Maybe this will help." He put a wooden box at the side of the horse.

"Can't it kneel down?" I asked.

"It's not a camel, Madam." The young man was getting a bit touchy. I climbed onto the box and he held the stirrup for my foot.

Sandy called out, "Go for it, Grandma, I've got the camera ready."

Henry gave my leg a boost; it helped, but it was a long way up.

"Now," the young man said, "put your right leg over the horse." The only way I could do this was by lying forward with my face in the horse's mane. I somehow managed to get my leg over, and young bossy shouted, "Now sit up," so I pushed as hard as I could.

"Have you been polishing this horse or something? It's very slippery," I told him as I finally managed to get into an upright position. Now I know what a wishbone feels like when you pull it apart.

"Hold it, Grandma!" Sandy was pointing the camera at me. The ground looked a long way down. Somehow I mustered up a smile. "Got it, Grandma!" Sandy said.

"Catch me," I shouted as I slipped sideways. Henry and the young man caught me and lowered me gently to the ground. Then Henry took the bridle and put his good left leg in the stirrup.

"Excuse me, sir," asked the young man, "do you intend to ride this horse or just sit on it?"

"Aye, lad," said Henry, "I'm going for a canter." He raised himself up, then leaning forward he swung his right leg over the horse. I walked round to the other side of the horse. The young man followed me. I'll never forget the look on the boy's face. I gave Henry's leg a hefty belt behind the knee. The young man stepped back as the leg made a loud 'click.' I then pushed Henry's shoe into the stirrup and winked at young bossy. He went pale.

The rest of the riders were now slowly moving off.

"Sandy," I called, "take a picture of Henry." For some reason my voice must have startled the horse. It lifted its two front legs and the young man danced to one side. Henry's face under his Stetson hat was ecstatic. He gave a 'whoop' and waved his free hand as Sandy took a picture. I blew him a kiss and he galloped off.

"He's just like John Wayne," I said. "Only Henry's galloping off into the sunrise."

July 6th

Arthur Proctor was standing in the doorway of his room this morning as I went by. I noticed that the wide parting created by the hairdressing student was now filling up with hair again. However, the new hair was standing straight up, while the rest was as usual, falling over like a dirty mop. He was leaning his skinny frame against the side of his open door wearing his best Hawaiian shirt. He wears it whenever his son Ronnie comes to visit. The shirt is covered with bare breasted hula girls wearing grass skirts and flowers round their ankles. He was also wearing the tie that he thinks goes with this shirt. It's black satin with a green crocodile smiling on the front, it even glows in the dark. Don't ask me how I know.

As I passed his door he said,

"About that form of yours…." Arthur looked me up and down in his usual sleazy, yet complimentary, manner.

"I beg your pardon, were you speaking to me?" I asked.

"Yes. I'd like to do something with that form of yours."

"You're disgusting, Arthur Proctor," I replied.

"No, no," he said, innocence pouring from his bright blue eyes. "I mean that funeral form you gave me. Come on in, Clover, I want to tell you about my burial."

"Well, I'm listening," I said from the middle of the hallway.

"I'm being buried at sea," he announced proudly.

"Oh, my," I said. "That's interesting." I found myself drifting into his room. With a deft move he kicked the door shut. He went on…

"You know, after the army I joined the Merchant Marines. The sea is in my blood, Clover. So I've decided it's a burial at sea for me." His blue eyes seemed to water. I walked a couple of steps closer. He had me hooked.

"That's quite romantic, Arthur," I told him.

"Yes…my son Ronnie's going to tip me off his yacht into English Bay. I'll be wrapped up in a flag." He wiped his eyes on the sleeve of his shirt. "I was hoping you'd be there, Clover, to sing that nice song…you know…'Red Sails in the Sunset'." I was now entranced.

"Well, I do have a good voice that would carry over the water," I told him. He unravelled some of the toilet paper he always carries in his front pants pocket. He blew his nose and dabbed his eyes. I heard footsteps. I opened the door and looked down the hall. His son Ronnie was coming toward us carrying two paper cups of coffee. I went to meet him.

Ronnie must be about six foot two standing up straight. His shoulders are rounded now. He's retired from the post office and looks as though he'd carried too many letters around in his time. Ronnie gazed down at me. His eyes are pale blue; they're like his father's but not half as brilliant.

"Hello, Clover you're looking…" I hadn't time for chitchat.

"That's a lovely burial you're giving your father," I told him. Ronnie's mouth opened but nothing came out. "He was just telling me. Imagine, you're going to drop him off your yacht into English Bay. And the wonderful thing is that he'll be wrapped in a flag. I think that's lovely." I noticed Ronnie's hands were trembling. He tried to hold the paper cups steady but some of the coffee bounced over the top. "I can see you're upset, Ronnie, at the thought of losing your dad."

"Oh, it's not that, you just caught me by surprise." Ronnie looked around and whispered as though delivering a secret code, "I don't have a yacht. I only have a small rowboat." I was taken aback.

"Well! Really! How can I stand up and sing, 'Red Sails in the Sunset,' when we're rocking in a rowboat?"

"What?" He spilled a bit more coffee.

"I've just had a last request from your father, Ronnie. He just begged me to sing at his funeral." It was my turn to dab my eyes with my hanky.

"I'd better go have a word with him," Ronnie answered. "You know sometimes I wonder about Dad's mind."

"I hope you haven't been paying attention to your father's psychiatrist?" I said, "Arthur is as quick-witted as they come, believe me."

"Yes...um...I'll just go and put him right about the...um... yacht, I mean the rowboat," Ronnie stammered.

"Yes, I think you should. You'd better get your act together, Ronnie," I pointed out. "Now if it happens we're stuck with just a rowboat, you know I don't have to stand up to sing. I can sing sitting down, I'm very versatile. Listen," I went on, "maybe we could get the...you know...the funeral people...to put your dad in a sitting position then, just as I come to the end of the song, you rock the boat and with a little push, over he goes..."

Some more coffee came splashing over the top of the cups.

"I wouldn't want to see my poor dead father sitting in a rowboat..."

"Well, you wouldn't see him, would you?" I reminded him. "He'd be wrapped in a flag. You know, Ronnie, these are things you should be sorting out before it's too late." Ronnie moved over to the window and leaned on the sill. "Your father's getting very frail," I told him, "especially as he keeps drinking that stuff that no one knows about in the bottom of his clothes closet." Ronnie tried to straighten himself but his hands still shook.

I walked off while he still had some coffee left. I looked back to remind him of some very useful information.

"Ronnie…flags are on sale at the Army and Navy store. It's a Canada Day special. You need one about as big as a tablecloth. You don't need to buy a pole."

July 7th

The Activity Department keeps coming up with ideas to stimulate our minds. They started a series of meetings today called 'Talk about.' When we got onto politics, it became a 'shout about.' Then I got really mad at Arthur Proctor when he said he thought a woman prime minister would be too soft. I hit him with my purse and it wound up being a 'roust about.' I'm banned from any more meetings.

As if I care.

July 9th

I'm going to give the Activity Department one more chance. I see they've got a notice up saying, 'Sign up for Creative Writing Classes.' It went on to say that a teacher would be coming from the university to give a summer course. I think I will be very good at this. I'm quite creative as long as I don't have to stick to the truth. I also must remember I was born in the same area as the Bronte sisters. I know I was sick of hearing about them at school.

July 11th

I had my first creative writing class today. About twelve of us showed up. I was surprised to see Arthur Proctor there.

"Well," he said, "it's either this or hymn singing in the chapel."
Our teacher is called Oscar De-Lamont. Ms. McPherson acted as

though he was royalty when she introduced him. She said he had a B.A. and an M.A. and a PhD. I bet he didn't have a J-O-B, that's why he's here. Ms. McPherson took ages telling us how wonderful he was.

"This young and gifted man has given up part of his vacation to impart his knowledge of creative writing to us." She said it as though she were going to sit through the whole thing with us. Oscar looked like a tall, puffed-up penguin. He wore a white shirt under a black waistcoat. You could have cut yourself on the crease of his black pants. His hair was smoothed back and glossy, as though he'd used black boot polish. I heard him mumble something to Ms. McPherson, something about, "They're rather older than I thought."

"Well," she pointed out, "this is an elderly facility, you know."

"Yes...but do people really live this long?" I admit three people on the front row were asleep. They'd been sleeping there since the slide show two hours earlier. The show was about 'Keeping Lamas for Fun and Profit.'

Oscar looked down at us from his more than six-foot height. This made his glasses slip down his nose. He pushed them back in place and waved a long arm.

"Hello," he shouted. We gazed back at him. He looked down at Ms. McPherson. "Are they deaf too?"

"No, we're not," I shouted back. "We're just waiting for you to say something worth listening to." Ms. McPherson raised her hand then pointed to Oscar.

"I give you Oscar De-Lamont, a 'published poet.' I will leave you in his good hands." She walked away.

For a moment I felt sorry for him. He looked like a kid whose mother had left him alone in a graveyard after dark. His hands were shaking as he held a small black book to his chest. He was a bit too young for my liking. I had someone in mind like George Bernard Shaw, with a nice long beard. I'll give Oscar a chance, though.

He started by telling us to draw from our lives for inspiration. "Some of you," he said, "may be budding poets."

I got a bit worried though. He read from his little book of poetry and none of it rhymed.

July 15th

I sat down today to write a story for Oscar De-Lamont. I think he's mistaken when he tells us to draw from our own lives. My life is too ordinary. I asked myself, what do people want? I couldn't think of an answer so I called my grandson Sandy. Being eighteen, he knows everything.

"They want excitement, Grandma," he told me. "And sex and money and a lot of high tech stuff, and violence and horror and nudity and…"

"I think I've got the picture," I said as I hung up. He was right. I now had something to go on. It took nearly two hours to write my story. I hope Oscar appreciates it. I can hardly wait till the next class.

July 18th

I went to my second writing class today. Nearly everyone had written something. I had to sit through a lot of very boring stuff, including a poem by the Dolly Sisters about their two goldfish dying. First of all they told us about the pet shop man doing an autopsy to see why the fish died. The poem was worse; they even handed out copies. The twins took turns with each line.

"The title is Bobby and Berty.

> Oh cruel fate why did our fish die?
> We saw their floating bodies and it made us cry.
> The pet shop man said we should not use tap water.
> 'Now,' he said, 'you see the slaughter.'
> Now we look into our lonely bowl
> And all we see is an empty hole.
> The mermaid and the lobster mourn.
> We wish that we were never born.

'Where are our friends?' they say quite vexed.
They're dead. We'll get some hamsters next."

The twins sniffled into their Kleenex tissues and sat down. Everybody clapped. Oscar De-Lamont looked at the twins for a moment. He didn't seem to know what to think.

"We feel your pain and sorrow...don't we?" he said to the rest of us. There was a shout from someone just then.

"What you two need is a couple of Guppies." It was Arthur Proctor. He came up to the podium with a sheet of paper in his hand. "You can put Guppies in soup and they won't complain." Arthur waved his paper at the teacher. Oscar consulted a list on his desk.

"Ah, Mr. Proctor, I believe."

"Yes. Now for something different," said Arthur. He had written a limerick. As might be expected, it was rude.

"There was a young lady from Kent.
She gave up her lover for Lent.
When she wanted him back,
he'd jumped in the sack,
with a girl who mistook what Lent meant."

Henry asked him for a copy. The teacher's eyebrows were still raised as he called, "Next please."

Henry went to the front. He read a lovely story about trying to get into the army and how disappointed he was when the recruiting officer told him he was at a disadvantage with having only one leg.

In between all the stuff we were reading, Oscar De-Lamont kept interrupting with little lectures on how we need truth and integrity in writing.

"Tell me about your lives," he kept saying. "Tell me what you are passionate about," he pleaded. That's a dangerous thing to ask with people like Arthur Proctor around. We just nodded our heads and listened. Finally it was my turn. I stood to read like everyone else at the podium.

"The title of my story," I said, "is... <u>Lust is a Many Splendored Thing</u>. The opening moments of my story find Deedry, my leading lady, relieving herself of her shimmering cocktail dress in the hothouse of her friend's garden, simply because she is hot. She is suddenly startled and finds herself gazing into the eyes of Hades, my leading man. He is handsome and virile but she doesn't know that he's an unfrocked priest. Savagely, hungrily, they make love..."

I stopped reading for a moment because I noticed the teacher had left his desk and was standing beside me. He was loosening his collar. As he pushed his glasses back he asked,

"Is anyone finding it a bit hot in here?" No one said a word. "Yes," he went on, "I thought you would agree...by the way, Clover, you do remember that I asked you to draw from your life?"

"Yes," I told him, "this is me...well, it's me under different circumstances."

"Well, let's hope," he remarked, "that next week your circumstances will have changed and your ardour will have cooled a little."

"Can I be first to read next week?" I asked.

"Maybe," he answered, "if you promise to get those two out of the hothouse." I did intend to have them in the greenhouse for at least half an hour more. But I decided to cut this scene short.

I'll save that amorous section for another story since I think it's far too good to waste.

July 25th

There was another creative writing class today. I was ready to get to the podium as soon as Oscar De-Lamont had made his opening remarks. But, just as I was about to go, Arthur Proctor beat me to it. I didn't mind too much because he was wearing his medals so I knew he was going to be serious. He stood to attention and saluted before he spoke.

"My title is... <u>Don't Join the Army Unless You're Barmy</u>.

We both were shot while holding a bridge,
just me and me mate, his name was Midge.
We beat the odds just us two kids.
Those officers are just like turds,
full of shit and fancy words,
everyone of 'em bloody nerds.
'Cut down the trees and make a camp,'
one officer shouted, I wanted to stamp,
then a tree fell on him and gave him a cramp.
He had me and my pal confined to barracks.
We were peeling spuds and scraping carrots,
and sorting the laundry and taking out maggots.
I got my 'dick' shot. I was mad.
They said 'you're Four F'. I said 'Is that bad?'
'It means you've effing had it lad...'
A lot of my friends in battle fell.
Midge, well, he went A W O L.
They made me talk but I didn't tell.
I get on with women. When I get undressed,
I show 'em my scar; they're very impressed.
I like it when they kiss me better best.
If you think you'll go, then just think twice,
there's rats and vermin and bugs and lice.
I tell you what…it isn't nice.
Have we made this world a better place?
Is it on its arse? or on its face?
But buy a poppy just in case."

He saluted again and sat down amid lots of clapping and cheers. Oscar and I got to the podium at the same time. I thought he was going to announce me, but instead he went on about people sinking into gutter language and using sloppy phrases. He said we should all improve our vocabulary.

"Get a thesaurus," he shouted.

"Aren't they extinct?"Arthur Proctor shouted back. I thought they were never going to shut up. As soon as Oscar stopped for breath, I began.

"Now you will remember that our lovers were in the hot-house." I looked at Oscar who had gone back to his desk and was drinking a glass of water. "Well, they're out of there now, but they are still madly in love. Their destinies are entwined forever. One day Deedry realized she would have to take Hades home to meet her family. How could she explain to her lover the unhealthy relationship between herself and her strange cousin Alfredo? And what about the bat collection pinned to the walls of Alfredo's mansion? And what about the other terrible secrets of Shriek House, the repulsive mansion where her and Alfredo, and the devilishly fearsome Aunt Skitsy, shared an abode?

Yes, several terrible questions must be faced. Like, why Aunt Skitsy is hated and feared in the village? And why does Aunt Skitsy never buy balls of wool but only skeins? Yes. Deedry must tell Hades about the devastatingly awful dungeons of Shriek House...the horrible treadmill...the seven lost souls made to walk round and round winding the horrible yarn for Skitsy. What will her lover say when he finds out what Skitsy is knitting with this diabolical yarn? God, he will faint with shock..."

I stopped reading and looked over at Oscar.

"Is that it?" he asked a bit too hopefully, I thought.

"No," I told him. "I stopped writing just there because I had no idea myself what she was doing with this yarn. I'll figure it out by next week."

"Well, Clover," the teacher said, "I must say you're taking us along a lot of different avenues. Next week I'm sure you will have a dynamic climax for us."

"Yes, I'll try to give you a good climax," I promised. Arthur Proctor fired a question at me before I could sit down.

"Was she sleeping with this cousin then?"

"No," I answered. "They were just unhealthy, that's all." Arthur never gives up easily.

"Those bats on the wall...were they alive? Or were they dead?" I thought for a moment. I had always believed in kindness to animals.

"They were alive," I answered. "They were just hanging, you see, by one paw...on little elastic loops...They were alright...you could see them fluttering." Arthur looked suspiciously at me. I went on quickly, "He fed them, you know."

"Don't bats drink blood?" Arthur shot back.

"Well, there you are, you see. I told you they were both unhealthy. I mean wouldn't you be unhealthy. Because of these bats, she and Alfredo had to have a blood transfusion every day." That kept Arthur quiet for a while. Hoping to take his mind off the bats, I said, "By the way did I tell you there was a moat with crocodiles floating in it? And I've changed the name to Shriek Castle." I was pleased to see a lot of faces light up. But Arthur wasn't ready to give up.

"Isn't it illegal to sleep with your sister?"

"She wasn't his sister. And he wasn't sleeping with her." I shouted at him. The Dolly Sisters started now. One asked,

"Why couldn't Skitsy wind the wool on one of those winders like they have in arts and crafts?"

"What was she making?" asked the other.

"You'll just have to wait to find out," I told them.

"Why was the priest defrocked, I'd like to know," Arthur Proctor asked. There was a chorus from the back.

"Yeah, why?"

"Why?"

"Well, you'll have to wait and see, won't you," I told them all. Oscar De-Lamont leapt to his feet.

"Yes, quite right, Clover. We must wait and see. Our curiosity knows no bounds. But first, may I give you some constructive criticism? This is not so much a story as a synopsis...."

"What's a synopsis," I asked.

"It's a story about sin." Arthur Proctor volunteered. The teacher smiled at him.

"Amusing, amusing...Now Clover, your point of view seems to need a little work, and your tense...."

"I know I'm tense," I replied. "You would be too with these characters running around in your brain." Oscar waved his arms trying to get the attention of people who were filing out.

"About next week... Please don't forget I want you to draw from your lives. To take me somewhere you have been. Henry, I was moved by your attempts to serve your country and how you were turned away. Arthur, I could feel your frustration at life in the army. Your writing had the ring of truth. But Clover...could we have reality? Please? Did you get the point of the sisters' poignant poem?" he went on. "The tragic death of their pet fish. They were sharing their lives with us. Just take me somewhere you have actually been, Clover."

As everyone moved out I reminded them all,

"Don't forget what he said, did you all hear that? I know where I'm going with my story next week." No one seemed interested. "I'm going to the Canary Islands," I told them. "I can't remember any canaries...but I'll think of something."

Oscar De-Lamont snapped his briefcase shut. He made a race for the side door. Shy, I thought to myself. Yes, this was a sensitive young man, excited by the creativity he had brought out in us.

July 27th

I heard Judy talking to Rhodena this morning.

"Give Mr. Proctor these pills, Rhodena," she instructed. "He's been restless all night so they tell me." Rhodena went immediately with the little tray she always uses for medication. Arthur must be sick, I thought. I'll investigate as soon as me and Henry get back. We're going to watch the dragon boats practice from Burrard Bridge. Yesterday we took the Dolly Sisters. They went into hysterics when they saw the dragon boats. They screamed,

"Loch Ness monster, Loch Ness monster."

We're going alone today.

July 28th

I called in to see Arthur today. If he's sick I must evaluate the situation and practice the words to 'Red Sails in the Sunset'. I want to be word perfect when we throw him into English Bay. His room was strangely quiet. I pushed open the door. Arthur was sitting up with three pillows behind him. He was reading *The Racing News*. He bets on the horses every Saturday. There was a strong smell that reminded me of my childhood. He put on a really sorry face when he saw me.

"Clo...ver..." he moaned, "I knew you'd come in my hour of need." He pointed to the bottle of camphorated oil on his night table. "You're just in time to give me a rub."

"By the smell of this room, you're already covered in the stuff."

"Well, Rhodena did put a bit on my back, but I really need a bit on the front too."

"You may have a bad chest, Arthur," I told him, "but you've still got two arms."

"Clover," he croaked, "I can feel my heart slowing down, come and feel it." I came a little closer. He tore off a strip of the toilet roll sitting on his bed and made a big commotion of blowing his nose and drying his eyes. He looked at me just like a Spaniel Cocker dog that knows it's about to be put down.

"I can see you've got a nasty cold, Arthur. I'll tell you what I'm going to do." He reached out his arms hopefully. "I'm going to speak to your son Ronnie. I'm going to suggest we do a practice funeral."

"I'm not that sick Clover…I just need some tender loving care."

"You need to be prepared for the worst, Arthur. Time is of the essence." I picked up the phone and dialled the number on the paper at Arthur's bedside.

"Hello, Ronnie," I said. "Have you got the flag yet? Ronnie, Ronnie, it's me, Clover." Finally, Ronnie spoke.

"Don't tell me Dad's…" Ronnie's voice was shaking.

"Well, he's not looking good, but then he never does."

"Let me speak to my dear old Dad," said Ronnie.

"This is no time for sentimentality," I told him. "Here's what we're going to do. We're going to the beach near Stanley Park. I'll get my grandson Sandy. He'll help you drag your rowboat down to the water. I think we can squeeze four people into it…"

"Well, only just, Clover…"

"There'll be me and Henry and you and Sandy, and of course the body wrapped in a flag. He'll be on the floor."

Ronnie interrupted again.

"What body? You said Dad…" I could see Arthur reaching out to me with the bottle of camphorated oil.

"Just a little rub, please, Clover…" Arthur pleaded.

"Shut up, Arthur," I said. "I'm discussing your funeral. Now, Ronnie, about the body in the flag,…" There was silence for a while. "I've got one we can practice on."

"I don't think I want to hear this, Clover. You're scaring me." Ronnie can be such a nincompoop.

"I have the perfect thing, Ronnie. The first aid people left behind one of the mannequins that they practice their resuscitation stuff on. I don't know why, but they called her Sally. She's falling apart a bit and was probably meant to go in the garbage, but I rescued her. She's in my closet. She'll do the job for our mock funeral." Ronnie sounded as though he was sobbing. Arthur was restless again.

"Do you mean my funeral, Clover?" Now he was sobbing too.

"I mean our funeral Arthur, don't be selfish."

"So, Ronnie," I said into the phone, "we'll see you tomorrow night at nine pm. There'll be the Dolly Sisters, of course, and I'm wondering about Monster…"

"He won't fit…He won't fit," Ronnie was stuttering.

"Don't be negative, Ronnie," I said. "They'll be on the shore waving farewell." I slammed down the phone.

July 29th

It's all arranged for tomorrow evening at dusk. I called Sandy and told him the whole plan.

"Awesome!" he said. Sandy and Ronnie will carry the rowboat to English Bay. Me and Henry will carry Sally the mannequin. The Dolly Sisters had to be invited but agreed to just come to the water's edge and throw flower petals at the boat. The back garden of Honeystone Mansion looks a bit bare I'm afraid, but protocol has to be observed; we needed the flowers. The twins wound up with a Safeway bag each full of flower petals and we added some shredded newspaper to make it go further. I had second thoughts about Monster. I was sorry not to have him along though. I had lovely visions of him carrying the 'body' down to the water, just like Frankenstein's Monster carried the body in the film. But Judy refused to let him out. I explained that I thought he might like to see the sunset on English Bay. She didn't go for it.

"I don't know what you're up to, Clover," she remarked. "When will you realize that no matter how hard you try, this man is never going to speak?" I headed sadly for the elevator. It felt like Judy had plunged a knife into my breast then screwed it round just for spite. She called after me. "To him a sunset is just a fried egg disappearing."

This woman has no heart.

July 30th

We all converged on the beach at nine pm. There were still quite a few people there. A man was playing 'The Blue Danube' on a mandolin. Ronnie and Sandy were following us; they had no trouble carrying the aluminium rowboat. Henry was causing a bit of a stir; people looked curiously at the body under his arm, especially being wrapped in a flag. Henry just smiled when someone asked, "Is there really a...you know...a body...inside that flag?"

The twins threw a handful of flower petals and shredded newspaper on top of the coins in the mandolin player's open music case. He kept on playing but at the same time, he gave the case an angry kick sending some of the coins and the petals jumping out. Quickly, the twins picked up the petals and whatever coins had jumped out and put them in their Safeway bags. I hurried the sisters down to the water's edge. It was a bit of a squeeze for me and Henry and Sandy and Ronnie to fit into the small boat. Ronnie kept going on about breaking some law or other. Henry managed to fit Sally, the wrapped-up mannequin, on the floor of the boat. I thought I had told Sandy the whole story, but apparently not. When I said we were doing a practice funeral and that we even had 'a body' he just went along with it. He's a great kid.

"Gosh, is that the body?" asked Sandy. I quickly uncovered the mannequin. She looked like something from a horror movie- one arm was hanging off, her head facing the wrong way, and she was an awful patchy colour. She had obviously hit the floor too many times.

"Awesome," Sandy remarked. A small crowd was still watching us closely.

"Where're your life jackets?" someone shouted. I saw two life jackets under the seat and lifted them up.

"Don't worry about us," I shouted, "we'll share them." Unfortunately, one fell into the water and floated away and

Ronnie gave a little shriek. I gave the other jacket to Sandy. Just then a helicopter flew overhead. I took that as a sign from heaven. With shaking hands Ronnie gave Sandy one of the oars. Ronnie took the other and we floated away from the shore.

The Dolly Sisters had taken their shoes off and were wading in the water as they threw petals around and shouted, "He's off to heaven."

"Yes, off to heaven."

As we moved further away from the beach we heard their tinny voices in the distance singing…"Row, row, row your boat gently d-o-w-n…."

We headed out into the deeper water. We rocked a bit because Ronnie kept forgetting to stroke with the oar. We could hardly see his face. He'd pulled his black woolly sweater up over his nose. He nervously peered around. Sandy did most of the rowing. After a short while I decided we had gone out far enough.

"Stop! We're there, Ronnie," I called out. "Drop the anchor, or whatever you do to stay still."

"There's no anchor in a rowboat, Clover," he grunted.

"Well, just sit still everybody. I'm now going to sing dear Arthur's favourite song, 'Red Sails in the Sunset'." I held out my arms to the setting sun. (Well, it had already gone down but there was a bit of pink in the sky.) "Now, as soon as I start singing you, Sandy and Henry, lift up the body and fling it overboard. Hang on to the flag, we'll need it again." Lustily, with a lot of feeling I sang, 'Red Sails…' The mannequin flew over the side. I was ready to proceed with the rest of the song when a bright light hit us. Something was coming toward us.

"God, we've been spotted," muttered Ronnie as he buried the whole of his head in his sweater.

"Awesome," said Sandy.

"What are you doing?" The voice seemed to be coming through a loudspeaker. As captain of our small vessel, so to speak, I felt that I should take over.

"We're just throwing a body into the water," I shouted.

"What? Don't move! You're all under arrest!" The boat came closer and we could see Coast Guard written on the side. The man with the most gold on his uniform was issuing orders and shouting something about 'fishing the body out.'

"What is the identity of the person overboard?" All my crew seemed speechless.

"Just Sally," I told them. "She was in very bad shape…"

"You mean she wasn't dead?"

"Well, she was never what you would call alive." Someone on the big boat was now holding a large pole with a hook on the end. I went on to explain. "The body we really intend to throw over is back in Honeystone Mansion. This is just a practice."

I heard a very gruff voice say, "Get 'em on board. They must be from a lunatic asylum." I thought he was unnecessarily rude. Just then the man with the pole lifted the mannequin from the water.

"Got it sir, got it. It's a big doll." Sally was hanging by one of her legs. One arm was now completely gone. I could hear a bit of sniggering going on behind the man with the pole. Shortly, the captain spoke again.

"Okay folks, you may think that's funny. You've wasted enough of our time." I was hurt by his attitude.

"I fail to see the hilarity of the situation," I pointed out. "I sincerely hope you will not fish out the real body that we will soon throw in the water." Being quite a good actress I came up with a realistic sob. It didn't seem to work. This man had no sympathy.

"That's it. You're coming with us."

For the third time the police brought me back to Honeystone. I didn't think our Coast Guard and our police force could be so dense. I explained things so clearly. As for that snitch in the helicopter, he'll get his I'm sure.

Two policemen sat with us in Ms. McPherson's office. They handed Sandy over into his parent's custody; something about his age. Gerty gave me a menacing look.

"I'll see you later, Mother," she hissed. As they went through the door, I could hear Sandy telling his parents, "You should have been there; it was awesome."

Henry sat politely smiling while I again explained the situation. Ronnie kept muttering. "I knew it was illegal. I told you, Clover, it's illegal." Ms. McPherson looked awful; she'd been dragged out of bed. It was now nearly midnight. Ms. McPherson never likes anything that I'm involved in. She's so unreasonable. She even sided with the police when they said I was guilty of public mischief. She asked them, with a hopeful smile, "Would there be any incarceration?" The policemen shook their heads. Then I thought she was going to faint when one policeman grinned and said,

"Mrs. Rayton, Clover tells us–and I'm sure she's joking of course, that there's another body here at Honeystone Mansion. Clover said..." he looked at his notes, "We intend to throw a... Mr. Proctor overboard later." Ms. McPherson laid her head on her hands. I think she was crying.

"We can see you're very tired," said the other policeman. Then I remembered something. Both the cops jumped to their feet when I said,

"There are two other bodies. They're on the sand at English Bay." Ms. McPherson made a sound like an elephant lifting its foot out of a mud hole.

Me and Henry shouted together. "The Dolly Sisters!"

The two policemen looked at each other. One officer asked, "Are they alive or dead?"

I knew he was joking but I told them, "You can judge for yourselves. These two ladies are from the *Twilight Zone*."

As we reached the front door, two other policemen came in, each holding by the hand a smiling Dolly Sister. They still carried their Safeway bags. Their identity bracelets gave anyone who bothered to notice the Honeystone address. Shouting, they ran toward me,

"Oh, Clover, when's the next funeral?" said one.

"Yes, we must do more funerals!" said the other.

August

Aug.1ˢᵗ

There was a hum of excitement in the air today as we gathered in the activity room for our writing class. Me and Henry sat together chatting, noticing who was carrying stuff to read. Oscar arrived and we got started. Henry told of how he lost his leg. I was so proud of him. Arthur Proctor got serious again when it was his turn to read.

"You want us to take you where we've been?" he said to Oscar, who looked a bit nervous.

"You want truth and reality?" Arthur didn't wait for an answer. He read from some rather messy looking papers, which looked a lot like the backs of the menus the staff hand out each day.

"This is called <u>Truth and Reality</u>." He waved the papers at Oscar and a couple of sheets fell on the floor. Oscar bent and picked them up. He held them by the corners as though they were very important evidence at a murder scene. Arthur snatched them and started again.

"The food here stinks. You could use the porridge they give you for cement. In fact, I've bunged up a couple of nail holes in my room with it. And the tea! Talk about witch's piss. And how about those boiled eggs they keep giving us? You can feel them fall down inside and nearly shake your balls off...and if you ever want your boots soled and heeled, just keep the liver they give you every Thursday."

He got a round of applause as he went to sit down. We had a lively discussion on how we should frame his piece and hang it up in the foyer. There were suggestions about using the copying machine at the front desk. Someone said we should send a copy to the local newspaper. We also decided to find out which penal institution Sidney, our real cook, is in. We thought we might plead for his return on medical grounds.

Oscar De-Lamont strode over to the podium. He blew a sharp blast on a whistle. None of us had noticed it hanging round his neck. His usually pale face was quite pink. We stopped talking and looked at him.

"Sorry...I find it hard to get your attention sometimes. Now Arthur, may I say something about your...piece of writing? While your words do have a startling reality about them, I do feel a bit of editing is needed. It has a...rough quality...which reminds me, I think it is your turn to read, Clover." I was already halfway to the podium. I don't like to waste the teacher's time.

"Right," I began. "This is <u>Lust is a Many Splendoured Thing, Part Two</u>."

"'Hades, my darling,' said Deedry as they stood in the conservatory of Shriek House, which is now called Shriek Castle. 'What is that in your hand, dear?' she asked as they watched the crocodiles swimming lazily round the moat.

'It is a letter from the Pope, dear,' he replied. 'He says he is sorry for defrocking me and wants to give me my frock back.' Deedry's heart was mixed with pleasure and pain at these words.

'How long do we have, darling, before you are once again a celibate priest?'"

I heard the teacher's chair scrape as he stood up.

"Pardon my interruption, Clover, but...um...didn't we talk of reality? Of things with which we are familiar?"

"I know, I know," I told him. "Just wait, it's going to get real, honestly, we're going to the Canary Islands where I've been."

He waved his arm. "Make it quick. Please," he said as he sat down.

"Okay, I'll speed it up a bit," I said. "So...they go to this banana plantation, which is in the Canary Islands," I looked over at the teacher, "where I've been, then they think of a plan to fool Skitsy and put an end to her terrible weaving..."

"You said she was knitting not weaving," one of the Dolly Sisters complained.

The other twin opened her mouth, I cut her off by saying, "Well, it was a mixture. There was even a bit of crocheting in there if you want to know."

"Tell us again, Clover," Henry asked. "Why were these 'lost souls' winding the wool on a treadmill?"

"Well, because she's got a bottle of poison rigged up on a pole and it drips a drop at a time on this wool..."

"But won't she get poisoned when she knits it?" one of the Dolly Sisters chirped. She nodded at the other sister, her silly curls dancing. I felt like banging their heads together.

"No, she won't," I said. "She's wearing gloves." I realized being an author wasn't easy. "Now," I said, "can we get on with the story?" I took a moment to find my place.

"Then Hades asked Deedry, 'What does she propose to do with this dastardly wool stuff that you were telling me about?'

'She is creating a huge spider web,' Deedry replied. 'And she intends to drop it on the nearby village.'

'Gad! What a ghastly woman she is,' Hades said. Then Deedry told him about her clever plan. 'We will send for Skitsy and Alfredo at the time of the locust.'"

"Locust?" It was Arthur Proctor again.

"Yes, locust," I shouted at him.

"Are they the same as grasshoppers?" I ignored him and went on reading.

"'Locust always attack the bananas in June...'"

"The grasshoppers attacked my corn in August," shouted Arthur.

"The locust always attack in June," I repeated.

"Grasshoppers attack in August,"

"Locust attack in June, Arthur, and if you don't shut up I'll attack you."

"Feisty little bitch isn't she?" he said leaning over and prodding Henry who smiled and nodded back. Just as I was about to start reading again there was another blast on the whistle. Oscar made no apology this time. He pointed to his watch.

"I'm afraid we're out of time, Clover. We will have to wait another week for the end of this...saga." I didn't mind stopping because my throat was getting dry.

As Oscar closed up his briefcase I reminded everyone, "Come next week for the thrilling end of my story." One or two people had fallen asleep; they woke when I raised my voice. "Hear about the devastation of the locust." I looked straight at Arthur Proctor as I said this.

"You want devastation," he said, "You should have seen my corn."

"I've seen you, Arthur," I told him as I headed for the door. "That's devastation enough."

Aug. 3rd

Snerdy Turdy will be up to see me shortly. There's a bit of damage in Maisey's half of the room. I broke her mirror and knocked the volume knob off her TV. I also broke two cheap little ornaments. Maisey said the ornaments were Royal Doulton.

"Oh," I asked, "has Royal Doulton opened up a branch in Hong Kong then?" Snerd will probably charge me extra because of the red blotch over Maisey's eye. She dodged when she should have stayed still and I accidentally hit her. I'm sorry about the bump on her knee where she fell...again. It all happened while I was chasing a hornet. Of course, what got Maisey really mad was the fact that I rolled up her *Sightings of Elvis* magazine to swat it with. Now she's not speaking to me again.

Next time I'll let the darn thing sting her!

Aug. 4th

Snerd came. He reckons I owe Honeystone Mansion thousands of dollars. He took out his notebook and reeled off some stuff. I carried on doing my eye exercises while he rambled on. Most people roll their eyes when they're in Snerd's company anyway, so the fact that I was doing eye exercises eluded him. He went on about nails in Monster's wall. He reminded me about the fire in the bathroom and the new dress he bought me because of the skunk. Some busybody told him I had clogged up the electric pencil sharpener at the front desk. I explained to him that now and then I needed a sharp point on my lipstick. I thought he was taking it all a bit calmly, and then he dropped the bomb.

"I'm putting you down for a visit to the psychiatrist," he said. I told him that no one was going to mess around with my mind. When Snerdy Turdy had gone, I decided I would tell the psychiatrist myself. I'll go to Arthur Proctor's room. Arthur sees the shrink every Monday morning. It doesn't do any good. Arthur is batty, that's just a fact of life.

Aug. 7th

I saw the psychiatrist in Arthur's room this morning. He's really nice looking. I've decided I might benefit from one or two intimate sessions with this man.

Aug. 8th

At creative writing class today quite a bunch of us showed up, mainly because I banged on all their doors as I passed. The Dolly Sisters had another boring poem.

"It's about leaves, Mr. De-Lamont," one of them told the teacher.

"Yes," said the other, "and they're falling."
As usual they read a line each.

> "The leaves are falling on the ground
> with a very quiet sound.
> Some are yellow, some are red.
> Some are a mixture, but they're all dead.
> We think we hear them sadly mutter,
> as they flutter in the gutter.
> We wonder if they ever care,
> when the man who sweeps them starts to swear."

They both giggled and smiled at the teacher before trotting back to their seats.

"Yes...quite lovely," Oscar said, "Of course you do impede yourselves when you insist on rhyming you know. However..."

I was surprised just then to see Henry stand up beside me.

"Yes, Henry?" The teacher looked pleased.

"I just have a very quick poem...I won't come up there," Henry nodded at the podium and went right on.

> "Throughout my life I've met some lasses.
> I guess I've made my share of passes.
> But when I thought my life was over,
> I met the best of all...and that is Clover."

He sat down and gave me a kiss. I don't often blush, but with all the clapping and silly noises Arthur Proctor was making I couldn't help it.

"Ooh, Clover's all red," one of the twins simpered.

"She's red as red," said the other.

"No I'm not," I told them. "I'm wearing Avon make-up. It's called 'bursting a blood vessel'." Henry gave me a hug. Oscar blew his whistle but not too loudly.

Of course, Arthur had to spoil the mood with another of his poems. He swaggered down to the front.

"Hello, everybody, and now we know who put the honey in Honeystone." He smirked at me and Henry. Henry laughed and waved at him. Arthur's title was nearly as long as his poem.

"The title is, <u>If you can keep your head when everyone else is losing theirs, then it shows you don't know what's going on</u>.

This country should be run by folks like me.
Folks that have a lot of sanity.
I'd invest the taxes in a really good thing,
down at the race track. I know who will win.
People should do what they darn well please,
like sing a few hymns or do a striptease.
I'm as sane as him, (he jerked his
thumb at Oscar De-Lamont)
so it makes me pissed when they make
me see the psychiatrist."

Arthur got applause as usual; he has a way of hitting the nail right on the head. The teacher raised his hands.

"Once again, Arthur, I must take you to task for your use of imprecation."

"Don't mention it," said Arthur as he went to sit down.

We then had to sit for half an hour and listen to Agnes Micklefield telling us how she rode across Indonesia on a Yak. "I wore a purdah," she told us.

"Is that like channel number five?" asked Arthur Proctor.

"No, it's a thing that covered my features. So no man could be tempted by my face."

"I wouldn't be tempted anyway," Arthur told her. Agnes ignored him.

Then she almost whispered. "I was twenty five at the time and unbelievably I was never once molested."

"Oh, I can understand that," Arthur chipped in. I couldn't help thinking that she certainly wouldn't be molested today, what with her five-inch jowls, plus a few moles, and quite a few whiskers. I don't want to be judgmental, but she looks a bit like a Yak herself.

"Spellbinding, simply spellbinding," said the teacher. He ignored the few people who raised their hands. They seemed to think it was their turn to read. I got to the podium quickly. Oscar looked at me and poured himself a glass of water. I faced my audience.

"Now," I said, "you all remember the beautiful Deedry and the handsome Hades?"

"And the locusts," shouted Arthur Proctor. I pretended not to hear.

"Well, now you will hear the thrilling erotic climax to this wonderful saga–" Just then the fire bell rang.

Oscar De-Lamont jumped up and in a strangely jolly voice he almost sang, "Fire bell, fire bell, that's the end for today." People were jostling to get to the door. Henry came and took my arm.

"There's always another time for your racy story," he said kindly as he gave me a squeeze.

I was angry though when I found it was only a practice fire drill.

I felt like setting a fire myself.

Aug. 10th

I'm getting bored with this funeral form job. I'm down to the last few forms, thank goodness. I didn't catch Nettie Spooner when I called last time but I found her in today.

"So, Nettie," I asked, "how are you? I notice your fan collection is back on the wall." Nettie was stitching one of her chiffon scarves; it was the colour of someone about to be seasick.

"Don't you love it, Clover? It's called meadow green." She broke off the thread and stuck the needle into the stomach of a stuffed poodle. It was balancing on two legs in a begging position on her dresser. She waved the scarf in the direction of my nose. I sneezed and decided I'd better get down to business.

"Nettie, management wants to know about your funeral arrangements. Here's a form, I'll help you to fill it in."

"I probably won't need a form, Clover," she told me as she waved her sickly scarf.

"Oh, you're going straight to heaven then?" I asked.

"Well, not exactly." She looked at me through the thin scarf. I realized I'd seen green faces like this on the Queen Mary when I came over to Canada. She peered over the top. "The university is coming to pick up my body. I'm leaving it to science." I sat down on the side of her bed.

"Nettie, have you discussed this with UBC yet?" I asked. "I mean...think about it, you're heart's on the blink, you've got arthritis and frankly, Nettie, I certainly wouldn't want your bladder. You've been wearing grown-up diapers for a long time."

"We are not talking about my bodily organs, Clover," Nettie walked around the room as she talked. She waved her scarf as though hitting invisible flies. "We are talking of my mind. I'm on a higher plane than most people you know, Clover." She did a full circle of the room then back to me. She swished the scarf at the top button of my blouse. I sneezed again.

"I must say, Nettie, I have noticed you're on a high plane sometimes. It's usually after your daughter brings those funny cookies. I've often wanted to know what's in those cookies, Nettie. And what is that green stuff all over them?"

"It's a very special herb, Clover. My daughter grows it on her balcony." Nettie wafted the chiffon scarf over the keyboard of her tiny organ.

"Well, I have to admire your daughter. Those cookies seem to give her a lot of courage," I said. "I heard on Sunday that she was in the male visitor's washroom. She was singing, 'I am Woman,

Hear me Roar.' They sent a male nurse in to get her out. She gave him quite a fight."

"Like myself, Clover, my daughter Desiree is very badly misunderstood." Nettie now tied the chiffon scarf around the trunk of a stuffed pink elephant. She placed it on the floor and pulled it along as she walked. It immediately fell on its side. Nettie sighed, "It has absolutely no sense of balance." She picked the elephant up by its trunk, twirled it a couple of times, flinging it onto my lap. I stood up, letting the elephant fall.

"Well, that was all very interesting, Nettie. Write it all down on the form. I know management will find it fascinating too. By the way, I'll take a couple of those cookies if you have some to spare."

I waited while she disappeared onto her balcony where she keeps the cookies in a tin box. Quickly, I picked up the stuffed elephant, the sick green scarf, and the poodle. I opened the top of the organ–everyone on the fourth floor hates her organ. Nettie knows just one hymn and we're sick of it. I had to hurry. I could see all the funny wooden things down inside that made the organ work. I squeezed the stuffed animals as far down as I could. The organ was now so full it was hard to close the lid. I said to myself the next time she plays 'Onward Christian Soldiers,' the soldiers will at least sound as though they're marching in their stocking feet.

Aug. 11th

I had some of Nettie's cookies for breakfast. I don't remember much about today.

Aug. 15th

It's Tuesday again. I felt sure I would be first to read. Oscar De-Lamont stood by the podium as though he were about to give another of his lectures. Before he could begin, we noticed someone floating from the back of the room toward him. She was wearing a long flimsy gown. It was Nettie Spooner. She ignored the teacher and held her arms straight out as though she was going to take off and fly.

"I feel the muse upon me," she said as she turned to face us. Her eyes were glassy. Oscar looked at his notes.

"I don't think I've had the pleasure," he said. Nettie didn't seem to see him. She tugged at the neck of her dress. A few of the pearl buttons holding the dress together fell to the floor. The left side of her dress slipped from her shoulder. Oscar's eyes darted to her chest. He reached out as though to hold up the strap of her dress. Nettie stood on his foot as he took a step forward. Oscar's yell was muffled by Nettie's high-pitched voice.

"Ah...the thralldom of catastrophic agony and pain.
The light, the light, shine the Utopia's light on me again.
All is not lost, oh denizens of these redundant shores.
Pick up thy transitory spear and aim it at the cause.
Poor mortals saliently cast in your mundane and trivial coil.
I am the force, the keeper of the self-explanatory spoil.
Come metaphysically through, I hear your infiltrating cries...
Oh, fly with me to rapturous, imperious paradise..."

"She's been at that funny stuff her daughter keeps bringing in," shouted Arthur Proctor. Oscar's eyes were misty—he dabbed at them with a large hanky. He came toward Nettie with arms outstretched as though to hug her. She stood perfectly still for a moment while some of us applauded, then she suddenly turned and flung out her arms, hitting Oscar across the face. He dropped his notes and while he bent to pick them up Nettie floated to the back of the room again toward the door. Oscar followed but with a neat flip of her foot as she passed through, Nettie tapped the door shut behind her. Unfortunately for Oscar, he walked right into it. When he turned round he had a strange look on his face, as though he had just seen a triple rainbow.

"There is a gem amongst us," he announced to the ceiling.

I was taken off guard so didn't rush to the podium as I should have. Then I was as surprised as the rest of the group when I saw who walked to the front. It was Ken Selacar. He hadn't read before; he is a rather shy man. His room is near mine on the fourth floor. Ken looked at the teacher.

"I am a rollicking buccaneer," he announced.

"Oh, really." Oscar didn't seem interested; he kept glancing at the door. Ken put a sheet of paper on the podium and read.

"I am a rollicking buccaneer,
I never have a bit of fear.
I go where brave men dare not tread.
I am invincible as well as well-bred.
I know I have goodness on my side,
and so into danger I will stride.
Solving crimes that are quite heinous
and crushing every evil genius.
Forget the Spider Man and Batman too
I am Australian, I jump like a kangaroo.
My strength is endless..."

Ken Selacar suddenly stopped and lurched forward. He grabbed the podium. The teacher jumped out of his chair, placed it quickly behind Ken and patted him on the back.

"Are you alright?" he asked.

Everyone shouted instructions. I got up and went to the door.

"I'll get help," I said. I stood in the doorway shouting, "Code blue, code blue," I happen to know this means someone has died...well...I know it means something serious. I knew I'd get action very quickly. Sure enough two care aides came from the fourth floor. They quickly put Mr. Selacar in a wheelchair and whisked him off to his room. Oscar wiped his forehead.

"I wonder if we've had enough for today," he said.

"No, we've got ten minutes yet," I pointed out as I ran up to the podium. "I know you are all dying to hear the end of my saga." A few people nodded and Oscar sat down. He made a noise like someone releasing the last bit of air out of a set of bagpipes. I quickly began reading before he changed his mind.

"Now...for those people who missed all the other exciting episodes, I'll fill you in. Our heroine is Deedry, beautiful and voluptuous. Our hero is Hades, handsome and everything. Now they have to get rid of Skitsy and Alfredo because one of them is a vampire and the other is killing a whole village with a big poisoned web. Now Deedry and Hades have to part because he has to go back to work for the Pope in Italy. He's a celibate priest at the Vatican. However he promises Deedry he will buy her a villa on the Isle of Capri and he will spend a sabbatical there every year–"

"Can we finish this off? Please, Clover." Oscar was looking at his watch again.

"Yes," I said, waving my papers at him, "here it is, the final conclusion of this tragic–"

"Please, Clover!" He picked up the whistle, but before he could get it to his mouth I took a deep breath and went on reading.

"So, they waited till June which was the 'time of the locust.' Everyone knows that locust love to eat banana plantations...then they tied Skitsy and Alfredo to a banana tree and hid in a ditch that had been sprayed for locusts..."

"Spraying didn't do any good for my grasshoppers," Arthur Proctor shouted.

"Shut up, Arthur," I said, without losing a breath. "Then when the locust had done their terrible work, Hades and Deedry made their last portrayal of passionate love among the debris. They could feel, smell, and taste the banana pulp under their hot bodies. Then, after their frenzied dance of love, Hades went to Rome where the Pope was waiting with his frock. So that's it."

Everyone applauded. I turned to look at Oscar De-Lamont. He was sitting at his desk staring straight ahead. He's enraptured, I thought to myself. He turned to me, and in a really quiet voice he said,

"I'm glad to hear the end of it, Clover."

"I thought you'd like the end," I replied. I was aware just then of the sound of crying. It was the Dolly Sisters.

"What about the lost souls?" one of them blubbered.

"The poor lost souls," whimpered the other. Oscar looked right at the twins.

"There are times, you know, when plots cannot be fully concluded. Shall we call it a day?" He stood up and shuffled the papers on his desk.

"Just a minute," I said tapping him on the shoulder. I could feel my public reaching out to me. I continued on.

"Right...well Deedry paid the lost souls a fantastic amount of money and she let them take the alligators to the everglades in Florida and set them free."

"What about the bats?" I knew Arthur would think of something.

"Does it really matter?" Oscar De-Lamont asked. He stuffed his papers into his briefcase.

"You know," he went on, "stories often have loose ends–" I interrupted him.

"I don't want anything loose in my story. Now, Arthur–the bats. Well, Deedry sold them to a movie company that specialized in Dracula movies."

"Oh, I see." Arthur was standing now with his hands on his hips, "I think I saw some of those movies." He shuffled to the door and a few others followed. I turned to look at Oscar De-Lamont.

"Boy," I said, "being an author really keeps you on your toes. Next week," I told him, "I'm going to take you somewhere real again."

"Well, Clover," he said, "my vacation from the university is nearly up. I'm not sure whether I'll make it here next week."

"Oh," I said, "I was hoping to take you on a weekend to Las Vegas before you left." He looked a little startled. "I'm going to tell you about the glitter and the shows and the stars, and the money I lost."

"Clover," he answered, "Las Vegas to me epitomizes all that is degenerate, decadent and dissipated in our lives today."

"Right," I said as I waved goodbye. I must write down some of those words to use in a story sometime.

Aug. 22nd

About the same group of people showed up for creative writing class again. We got restless as two o'clock came and went. There was a murmur from us all when our director Ms. McPherson came in. She stood at the podium.

"I'm sorry to have to tell you," she announced, "that Mr. De-Lamont will not be here this week. He finds that he needs a short holiday before going back to his studies. He did tell me he found the whole experience...mind-boggling...were words he used. He also told me he has decided to teach a younger group of students. It was quite taxing, he pointed out, to teach the very old. However, he will never forget his time here, he tells me." She smiled and waited for applause. None came. "Now, may I suggest we all move over to the multi-purpose room where the activity aides are making lovely serviette rings out of used toilet rolls?"

Everyone muttered a while then headed for the door. Ms. McPherson rushed ahead of us. She stood at the door as we filed out. Every alternate person got a kiss and a "My, you're looking well." I've seen her do this to people who've died two hours later. As I walked passed her I had something to say. She had just finished kissing the Dolly Sisters...they count as one.

"It's alright," I said, "about not having a teacher. Let's face it, this young man taught us everything he knows. I was thinking of branching out anyway." I went on, "You know...giving my own lessons."

"I see, Clover," she said. "Your self-assurance always amazes me." I walked passed her.

"Come on into the lounge everybody," I beckoned. "You can read your stuff and I'll read you my Las Vegas weekend saga."

"Did you see any nude shows?"

"Yes, Arthur," I said. I was lying but I could make something up. We settled in the lounge. No one offered to read so I got started. "This is called My Trip to Las Vegas." I began reading but I hadn't even got off the bus at Las Vegas before nearly everyone had fallen asleep. The sofas in the lounge are just too comfortable; even Henry had fallen asleep beside me. Only me and Arthur Proctor were wide awake. He was getting restless though.

"I'm going for a cig," he said as he headed for the smoking room.

"That's a pity, Arthur, because I was going to answer your question about why Hades got defrocked."

"Right-ho." He sat down again. "Go on, I'm listening."

"Well, it was St. Patrick's Day at the Vatican. Hades and the other priests all had some green jelly stuff for desert. Hades spilled some down the front of his frock so he went to the bathroom to clean up. There he was in just his underpants...they had little shamrocks all over them, when in walked a Cardinal. Cardinals have seniority, you know, and wear lovely red dresses. That's why those red birds are called Cardinals."

"I didn't know that," said Arthur.

"Well...I guess that's the reason, anyway," I went on. "This Cardinal sees Hades with his young, naked, virile body sponging off his frock by the sink." Arthur wiped some drool from his chin with the back of his hand. "And the Cardinal walks toward Hades with his arms outstretched like this, and says, 'You are mine.' Hades drops his frock and runs." Arthur thumped his fist onto his knee and laughed. I ignored him. "Now," I said, "who should be coming out of a nearby room just then, but the Pope. He sees Hades in his underpants and calls after him, 'If that's how you want to behave, just keep right on going out the door,' and that's what Hades did."

"Crikey," said Arthur, fumbling for his cigs again.

"Later of course," I continued quickly, "the Pope found out. The Cardinal had to say a lot of Hail Marys and flagellate a lot."

"What?"

"Flagellate. It has something to do with a whip."

"Crikey." Arthur wiped away a bit more drool.

"Now remember, this is between you and me. Some of these folk," I nodded at the dozing people around us, "don't understand the subtle aspects of life the way we do."

"No, that's right," said Arthur. "Not everyone would know this Cardinal was a fairy."

"Don't give fairies a bad name," I told him, "I was brought up on fairies. There are Fairies at the Bottom of my Garden was a favourite poem of mine."

"Well," said Arthur, "I'm telling you this chap was just like Basil Fairweather on the third floor."

"Do you mean I've been wasting my time being nice to Basil Fairweather? I didn't know he has homosexual tendencies," I said.

"There you go," said Arthur. "Now look at me. What you see is what you get." He slid over and put his arm round my shoulder. I looked at him.

"I'm not crazy about what I see, and I don't see anything I want to get," I told him. He shrugged and took out one of his homemade cigs. Bits of tobacco from his pocket sprinkled over my knee. Quick as a wink, he reached down and brushed his skinny fingers over my legs. I slapped his hand and he put both arms in the air and grinned.

I realized I was getting sleepy like the others. I was relieved to see Arthur shuffle off to the smoking lounge. About an hour later I woke up with my head on Henry's shoulder. I could hear the sound of teacups rattling; Kalmut was handing round the afternoon tea.

Aug. 28th

Arthur Proctor's composition about the food got us all thinking again. I have to admit that I actually had to tell a few people what to think. So we've signed a petition. It's called the <u>We Want Sidney Back Petition</u>. I wasn't sure which Ministry to send it to, so I got my grandson Sandy to send a copy to The Ministry of Health and Welfare; after all, this stand-in cook, Lorylee, could poison us before long and that would affect our health. The other copy I thought should go to the Minister of Family Affairs, after all Sidney does have a family. He has two in fact, which proves he's been having some family affairs. If they don't act on this humanitarian plea for help, I shall start sending parcels of Lorylee's boiled eggs, along with her leather fried liver, to the prime minister. I'll send them on a regular basis. And he better not think I'll bother with postage stamps either!

Aug. 29th

Today I took a stroll along Davie Street. I gave a quarter to the old man singing Christmas carols outside the SuperValu store. I explained to him again what time of year it was. As usual he took off his cap and said, "Seasons Greetings, Ma'am." I gave a lecture to the young woman holding out her hand near the video store. She had a kitten on her lap and a large dog beside her. The dog was wearing a striped cotton neck scarf. I told her the dog looked warm and the cat looked thirsty. She told me I looked like an old cow. I find this type of exchange of information goes on all the time as I walk around this interesting town of ours.

I crossed over Davie Street to the Park Hill Hotel where I noticed an empty police car sitting at the front door. I could hear a voice coming from inside the car but no one was there. I could see something that looked like a cell phone lying on the passenger seat. It seemed to be crackling. I love police shows on TV so I stopped to listen through the open window of the car.

"Come in, Jerry...Jerry. Come in, Marty...surely one of you is there," said a woman's voice from the other end. Now it was obvious to me that a crime was in progress. Why else would Jerry and Marty rush off in a hurry like this? I knew they must be in the Park Hill dealing with some dangerous criminal. They probably needed *back up* as they say on TV. I reached into the police car and picked up the cell phone or whatever it was. The woman repeated again.

"Jerry...Jerry...Marty,"

"Hello, hello," I said. She didn't answer, I looked at the phone; I was doing something wrong. I pressed the only button I could find. "Hello, this is a concerned citizen," I announced.

"What?" She had heard me.

"Jerry and Marty are not here right now, they're in the Park Hill...the scene of the crime."

"Who's that? Who's that?"

"My name is Clover Rayton. I am a dutiful citizen stepping into the breach as it were. Jerry and Marty need help. They are in the Park Hill...the scene of the..." The line went dead. I put the phone or whatever it was back on the seat and waited a while. Soon a young policeman came hurriedly out of the hotel. I had to move to let him into the car. Another policeman appeared from across the road eating a Mars bar. The radio crackled again and the first officer picked it up.

"Hi...what? Yes, sure I'm alright. No...I just had to take a shi...I needed the washroom real quick...it's my wife cooking. What? Yes, Marty's right here." Jerry and Marty looked at each other for a second; then both of them looked up in surprise as two police cars came round the corner from Thurlow Street with their sirens shrieking. Another car came up to the back of them from Bute Street. Then a truck stopped alongside them. Bomb Squad was written on it.

"Shit," said Jerry. Marty had dropped his head on the steering wheel. I heard the sound of a fire engine just then and thought to myself what a wonderful group of government employees we have in this town, to respond to our needs like this. It made me feel good and safe as I headed back to Honeystone Mansion.

Aug. 30th

The administration people at Honeystone have made another baffling decision. They are going to pay for Lorylee, our temporary cook, to have French Cuisine lessons at the community college. They have discovered something unbelievable. The cooking credentials she showed them when she came here for the job were obtained through a correspondence course.

Seems to me the post office has a lot to answer for.

Aug 31st

My son Horace phoned me today. He asked how I was doing, and if I was behaving. I wondered if they'd told him about the skunk, and the bathroom fire, and a few of the other little things. It looked as though they'd kept him in the dark because he sounded cheerful.

"There's a holiday weekend coming up," he said. "We thought you might like a change. How would you like to come and have a day with each of us? You could come to me and Tilly this Friday, and then to Muriel and Ben on Saturday. Doris and Tom would love to see you on Sunday, and Fred and Gerty will have you on Monday, Labour Day. We'll sort of spread you out between us."

"That sounds nice," I said. "I wonder why I feel like a jar of Cheez Whiz?"

"Okay," he said, "we'll pick you up after lunch Friday."

"I'm dizzy just thinking about it," I answered.

September

Sept. 1st

As arranged, Horace and Tilly came at two o'clock to get me. As we were going past the reception desk, Diane was making an announcement over the intercom.

"Don't forget to come to activities at three," she was saying, "for lessons in Chinese knot tying." I leaned over the desk and said into the mike,

"Bye Henry, see you in a few days." Diane pulled the mike to her chest as though it was a baby about to be kidnapped.

Horace and Tilly live in an apartment in False Creek. We sat on their sunny balcony after supper and chatted. I told them about Henry and the Dolly Sisters and Monster. I was about to tell them that I had begun to feel almost at home in Honeystone Mansion, when I noticed they had both nodded off to sleep. My God, I thought, they're barely sixty years-old and they're falling asleep in broad daylight. I stood at the balcony railing watching the people pass by. Soon I noticed an old man come round the corner. I watched as he put a grubby sheet on the grass edge just across from me. He dropped a few items on the sheet and I realized he was setting up shop. When a couple of young women walked toward him, he pointed down at the sheet and mumbled something to them. They paid no attention.

"Only a dollar," I heard him call after them. They still ignored him. He was doing it all wrong. I reached for my sweater and went down in the elevator. I crossed the road to the old entrepreneur.

"You've got to be aggressive in this line of business," I told him. "You've got to sell yourself." I looked more closely at him. I had to admit that if he was up for sale I wouldn't be buying. He was pathetic. His wrinkled old raincoat looked slept in, his pale blue eyes were runny, he kept moving from one foot to the other as though his feet hurt.

"Look, lady," he glanced up and down the street. "I'm trying to make a living. I'm not running for parly-a-ment."

"Let me see what you're selling here...what's your name?" I asked.

"Joe," he said. He almost toppled over as he bent to lift a couple of the packages from the dirty sheet. I took them out of his hand. They were pantyhose.

"How much are they?" I asked.

"A buck," he answered. I waved them in the air and took a deep breath and shouted,

"You'll never get a better price than this." A man and woman just about to pass stopped. Three people from across the road came over. "You'd better get them while they're hot," I said.

"Sh...sh..." Joe put his finger to his lips. He was doing a little step dance.

"Watch and learn," I said as I showed the packages to the five people clustered around. "The fantastic price of these, just for today mind you, is five pairs for...are you ready for this? Five dollars." Someone handed me a five-dollar bill.

A young girl turned to her friend and said..."Let's share some." She turned to me and asked, "Can we have six pairs for six bucks?"

"You're really asking me to bend the rules," I told her. "But here goes." Business was really brisk for half an hour or so. I was just handing Joe another five-dollar bill when a police car came round the corner and stopped at the curb. Two policemen got out.

"Okay," said the first officer, "where's your vendor's licence?"

"Oh," said Joe, "I'll just go and get it." With that he picked up the four corners of the sheet, stood for a moment swaying, then saluted and ran off like a jackrabbit.

I stood passing the time of day with the young officers for a while. I told them what a comfort it was to see a policeman now and then.

"Your mothers must be very proud of you..."

"He's not coming back is he?" one of the policemen interrupted.

"I've no idea," I answered.

"Look," said his partner, "we haven't time to mess about, either you tell us your partner's name and address, or you're coming with us."

It was a lovely afternoon for a drive. As we went over the Burrard Bridge, I could see sailboats and kayaks on the glistening water. We rode along English Bay where I could see people walking on the sea wall. It would have been even nicer if they had put on the siren, still it was exciting enough. I wasn't sure why they were doing a tour of the city, but it was very nice of them. As we drove around, the two policemen argued about who was to do the 'boring paper work.' Well I thought if they were going to write stuff down, it should be interesting. So I leaned back and told them the story of my life.

I got up to the present year. I was ready to tell them how my sons and daughters had had me incarcerated. I leaned over and showed them the bracelet on my wrist with Honeystone Mansion's address on it. There was a screech of brakes as the car stopped and made a U turn.

"Why didn't you tell us your address was on your wrist?" one officer said.

"Yes, for God's sake why didn't you?" asked the other.

"Well," I replied, "you didn't ask me, did you?" To my surprise, it wasn't long before we arrived at Honeystone Mansion.

"Look, lady," one of the policemen said, "we're not going to make a big deal out of this. We can't find your partner."

"But," said the other policeman, "you're obviously not a bad person. You just got into bad company." As he spoke he hurriedly got out and opened the back door for me. "So you can go home now." He nodded toward Honeystone.

"Oh, no, you've made a mistake." I explained that I was on parole as it were, and that my son and daughter-inlaw would be wondering about me. "But they don't live far from here," I said. The policeman who was driving looked at the other one. He hit the steering wheel with his fist.

"Get in, Charlie." His partner got in beside him. He leaned forward and touched the dashboard several times with his forehead. I thought to myself, these poor men are tired and ready to go off duty.

We had another nice drive around while I tried to think which of the buildings belonged to Horace and Tilly. It was getting dark and this made it more difficult, then suddenly it came back to me, even the number of the suite.

One of the policemen came with me, right up to the apartment. Horace's face was white when he saw me with the policeman.

"I believe this is your mother, sir?" the officer said.

"Yes. What's she been up to?" mumbled Horace.

"They caught me soliciting...." I told him.

"What?" Horace grabbed the side of the door. The policeman saluted.

"Just keep an eye out in the future," he said. He sounded very tired. He turned and nodded at me and left. I noticed Tilly; she was down the hall leaning on the kitchen door trembling.

"We thought you'd fallen over the bloody balcony, Mother Rayton," she said. "We nearly called an ambulance."

"Come and have some tea, Mother," said Horace. "Then we'll drive you over to Muriel and Ben...it's their turn next, you know."

"Yes, it's their turn now," Tilly chimed in.

"Oh, yes, I remember," I said. "You have to spread me around, don't you?"

I'd hardly finished my tea before they were racing me in the car to the outskirts of town. They had to wake me up when we arrived at Muriel and Ben's. I couldn't help thinking that a cup of cocoa with Henry at Honeystone would go down nice just now. Muriel answered the door. She was in her dressing gown.

"What time do you call this?" she asked. Horace opened his mouth to speak. "I don't want to know," Muriel blurted. She gave me a peck on the cheek and turned back to Horace and Tilly. "Just put her in the small bedroom upstairs, I'm going back to bed." Horace carried my suitcase upstairs. He gave me a hug.

"Well, it was nice knowing you," I said. I tried to be jocular but I was too sleepy.

"Good night, Mum," he said. He ran down the stairs. It was as though he had just set off a time bomb and had two minutes to leave the premises.

Sept. 2nd

I had to really stop and think where I was this morning; it was so quiet. I missed the sound of Maisey snoring in the other half of the room. I couldn't hear the noise of traffic coming from Robson Street. It was daybreak and the care aides should have been coming on duty; and why, I wondered, wasn't there the usual smell of burned toast coming from the Honeystone kitchen? I also realized that not one person had woken me through the night to find out if I was sleeping. I found myself hoping that the rest of the day would not be this boring.

I looked around and realized I was in the quiet, posh subdivision of my daughter Muriel and her husband Ben. They were still sleeping in the master bedroom next door. I put on the crème-coloured silk housecoat that was hanging on the back of the door. Muriel brought it back from Japan last year. I quietly went downstairs. Sammy, the cat, came from his wicker basket to meet me. As though reading my mind, he led the way to the kitchen.

Muriel's kitchen is so clean and sterile you could perform an operation in it. She also loves gadgets. I don't know what most of them are used for. I pushed a few buttons and got a few strange noises. Then I spotted something I understood, the blender. I had one of those myself once.

"Do you fancy eggnog, Sammy?" I asked. Sammy swirled in and out of my legs, as though he knew breakfast was on the way. "I think I remember the ingredients." I threw two cups of milk and two eggs into the blender. "Of course you know, Sammy," I explained, "it should really have half a cup of rum in it too; however, Muriel says no drinking till sundown. It's one of her house rules." I found a small jar of vanilla in a fancy wooden rack on the wall. I shook it to get the last few drops out and the jar fell into the mixture. I fished around for it, but before putting it back on the rack I let Sammy lick it fairly clean. He purred and scratched at the bottom of the silk housecoat. I bent down to unpick his claws; there were just a few little holes there, nothing much. I threw a handful of sugar into the blender and flipped the switch.

I gave a little shriek. Sammy leapt onto the countertop. I realized I had forgotten to put on the lid of the blender. Why doesn't it say in large letters on the front of the thing 'don't forget to put on the lid?' I danced back to avoid the drips coming off the ceiling. As the first drops fell on Sammy's head he hissed, leapt down, and latched on to the bottom of the gown again. I shook him free and turned off the switch. The tiny holes Sammy had made in the dressing gown were now small rips. I poured the bit of eggnog that was left in the blender into a glass. It was good, but as I reminded Sammy, it would have been better with some rum. I lifted the cat back onto the counter. He cleaned up the outside of the blender and the pool underneath it. Sammy must have liked it a lot. He let me hold him up while he licked most of it off the wall. I thought about the ceiling but it would have meant standing on a chair and holding Sammy upside down. I knew one of us would wind up with a broken leg. I left Sammy licking the trickles running down the kitchen cupboard.

It was six am. I went back upstairs and dressed. Muriel and Ben were still sleeping. I put the wet dressing gown into the laundry hamper. I could smell the vanilla, and I was glad I hadn't used a half cup of rum. The bedroom overlooked their back garden. Looking down I could see a large enclosure. I was puzzled at first; then I remembered they had a beautiful Red Setter dog. Dogs love company, I said to myself, I went down to say hello. A wire mesh fence surrounded the enclosure. Written above the huge doghouse inside the fence was her name, Boadicea. She stared beseechingly at me through the wire door. She whined softly.

"Wanna' go for a walk, girl?" I asked. The dog knew exactly what I meant; she practically tried to open the gate with her nose. It was a tricky latch but I got it open.

The dog came bounding out and pranced around the garden. I went over to the small shed to look for a leash. Inside, I had to move a lot of tools and things from the shelves. I finally found some thick string and decided that would do. I forgot where all Ben's tools and stuff went, so I left them in a pile in the middle of the floor. I had to smile when I went back to Boadicea. She was holding a dahlia as big as a saucer in her mouth. She laid it at my feet. I stuck the stem into the soil beside some pansies and hoped no one would notice.

I fastened the string onto Boadicea's collar and opened the back gate. I let the dog make her mind up which way we should go. The back lane led eventually to a small park. Boadicea bounded over to a pond in the centre. For a moment I lost the end of the string, but I caught up with her in time to stop her from heading to the middle of the pond to retrieve one of the ducks swimming there. Pretty soon Boadicea was sitting beside me chewing on the lower branch of a tree. I basked in the sun that had just risen and in a short while I fell asleep. I woke to find Boadicea wagging her tail beside me. I noticed one or two other dogs had appeared, and soon more joined us. I wondered what time it was and how long I had been asleep. I suddenly realized I was feeling hungry. Surely it was time for Boadicea to eat, but she seemed quite happy to be with the other dogs.

"Let's go home," I said, tugging at the leash. All the other dogs seemed eager to go with us. When we got out onto the lane I felt a bit like the Pied Piper. At least six dogs were trotting behind me. Looking down the lane I saw two figures approaching. I was surprised to see it was Muriel and Ben coming to meet us. They were in a big hurry. Muriel screamed at the sight of us.

"God look at her! She's a mess. Is she alright?" I was a little disappointed to find that she was talking about the dog. Muriel and Ben glared at Boadicea as though she had suddenly sprouted horns.

"Look how happy she is," I told them. "Look at her, she's almost grinning."

"I'm looking at her," said Ben. "And I'm not smiling."

"I suppose she needs a wash and a comb," I said. "But look at her, she's...happy." Ben turned to vent his wrath on all the strange dogs that circled us.

"Get home, you bloody hounds," he shouted. He even picked up a stone and flung it, "you four-legged bastards." The dogs fled. I could feel Boadicea shaking as she took refuge against my legs.

"Well," I said to Ben, "you woke up on the wrong side of the bed, didn't you?" Muriel was crying. She's good at that.

"Just tell me one thing," she asked. "Did you let her go?"

"Well, a dog has to go you know," I said. "Of course I let her go. It's only human for a dog to go." Muriel made choking sounds.

"She's ruined," she said.

"No she isn't, silly," I told her. "Those burrs will soon come out and she'll be like new again." I patted Boadicea's head.

"Did she do anything?" asked Ben. He sounded desperate.

"Let's see..." I tried to think back. "Why are you worried about little details like that?" I asked. Ben looked as though he was going to have an epileptic fit.

"That dog," he sputtered, pointing at Boadicea, "is slated to be mated to a thoroughbred Setter this week."

"Well whooptedo," I said.

Muriel dried her eyes. "What's done is done," she said. "Let's go home."

"Good idea," said Ben. "But to set our minds at ease, dear, why don't I take Boadicea to the vet after lunch to get her checked out—and I can drop your mother off at Doris and Tom's at the same time?"

"I thought I wasn't going to visit them till tomorrow morning," I said.

"Ah, well..." Ben looked at Muriel. "We're going to be a bit busy."

"Yes, Mother," said Muriel, who can be very sarcastic when she wants to be. "We'll be spending a bit of time removing stuff from the kitchen ceiling and the walls."

Doris and Tom were just having lunch when we got there. They looked a little taken aback. They gave me a hug and a cup of tea.

"We didn't think we'd see you and Mum till tomorrow afternoon," said Doris. "It's the peace march in the morning you know; we always do the peace march every year."

"Well," said Ben, "you can do the peace rally with Mother tomorrow. We've just done the war dance with her today." I told them to argue quietly and poured myself another cup of tea. I helped myself to a few Cadbury chocolate fingers. The four of them wound up in the front garden. I sat contentedly with my tea. I could see them waving their arms at one another.

Muriel seemed to be saying over and over. "Never again, never again." I heard Ben say, "Well, goodbye and good luck." And they drove off.

Sept. 3rd

I wasn't sure again where I was when I woke this morning, but then Doris came in with a cup of tea and a banana and I knew we were in West Vancouver at their home.

"Hurry up, Mum," she said. "We're off soon." I hadn't a clue where we were off to, but I love surprise trips.

It was a lovely day for a trip. We went through the British Properties, then over the Lions Gate Bridge. We had driven a little way onto the bridge when we came to a standstill. The traffic had been halted in both directions.

"I hope we're not going to be late," said Doris, "I hate missing the dignitaries; they always let them in first."

"It's probably just a minor accident," Tom said. "They'll tow them away in no time."

We sat for a while but then like many of the other drivers and passengers, we decided to get out and investigate. About halfway across the bridge we could see what the trouble was. An ambulance, three police cars and a fire engine were parked there. It was impossible to cross the bridge either way.

"What's going on?" Tom asked the nearest officer.

"We've got a jumper," he answered nodding his head at a skinny young boy standing on the railing of the bridge. My heart took a lurch as I saw him. He couldn't have been more than sixteen years old. He was waving one arm and holding on to the side of the bridge with the other. A couple of policemen stood listening to him as he shouted at them. A policewoman standing a little back spoke into a cellular phone. When Doris saw the young boy she gave a shriek. Tom shouted over.

"Get down...you crazy kid."

The policeman shook his head and touched Tom's shoulder. "You can make it worse you know, best leave it to us."

As I gazed at the young boy I recalled a movie I had seen a long time ago. The movie had a scene exactly like this; even the words used in the movie came back to me. Yes, it was quite clear now. It worked then, it would work now.

"Let me get a little closer," I said as I pushed between Doris and Tom. Doris tried to grab my arm.

"Don't interfere, Mother. Please...Mother!" I walked up beside the two policemen who were facing the boy. They seemed to have run out of words. A woman officer spoke in a hushed voice over a phone. The boy had turned. He was now facing the water. When I spoke, the two policemen turned my way as though both their heads had been jerked by a piece of string.

"Hey!" I shouted, "Get down from there immediately." The boy almost slipped then steadied himself. He turned and looked at me.

"Who the hell are you?" he asked. One of the cops seemed about to say something but hesitated as I shouted back.

"I'm your Mother!" I could hear Doris and Tom protesting in the background and someone telling them to shut up.

"You're not my mother, you old idiot." This wasn't quite the way the movie went! I would have to make up my own script.

"Just you watch your mouth, young man. You put these years on me. I'm your mother and I'm telling you to get down off there."

"Look, you interfering old bat," he shouted, "my mother's thirty-nine years-old and she's got red hair. And she wears earrings down to here." He let go for a moment and put both hands onto his shoulders, teetered and then grabbed quickly at the side of the bridge again. I shouted back.

"Well, that's what I looked like when you left home."

"What do you mean? I just left home three days ago." The boy looked around at the small crowd. "She must think I'm an absolute idiot." He looked at the nearest policeman. "She's lying!"

"Now is that nice?" the policemen said, then turning to me whispered, "Are you sure you're not his grandmother?" I was busy thinking of the rest of the script. It was coming back. I pointed to my face.

"This is what worry can do, you know." I moved a little closer to the young kid.

"My hair turned gray overnight. It's all the stress you're putting me through. I mean...look at you...I spent well-earned money on you and look at your torn pants." The boy looked down. His jeans had holes in the knees and thighs.

"If you were my mother, you would remember, you bought me these jeans, they're designer jeans." He slid his hand across his face as though wiping away tears. "Oh, yeah...it was well- earned money alright...money she got after midnight on Granville Street." I tried to think where on Granville Street anyone would be working after midnight.

"Well, I could always change my shift, you know," I said hopefully. This was the moment in the movie when the boy got down from the bridge railing and ran to his mother, put his arms round her and said he was sorry. Instead this kid looked desperate and beaten. He closed his eyes and turned again to the water. I had to give it one last try. I moved closer.

"Come and give your mother one last kiss before you go to your death." I held out my arms. Once again he turned.

"For the last time!" he shouted. "You are not..." he lifted both arms in the air letting go of the girder. He over-balanced and for-tunately fell forward. Two of the policemen quickly caught him. They restrained him as he made a lunge at me. All four officers surrounded him.

"Easy boy, easy boy," one of the officers said.

"Okay! Okay! Let go!" the boy said, "I don't want to kill myself anymore, I want to kill her." Doris was now standing with her arm around me. I could hear the woman officer speaking into the phone.

"It's over, it's over. He's off the edge." Two of the policemen walked him quietly to the police car. I looked for the last time at the boy.

"I could have been your grandmother," I called after him. He looked defiantly at me, which I thought was healthy.

"Well, you're not! What you are, is a mother-" the nearest policeman put his hand over the boy's mouth.

I stood daydreaming for a moment till I was aware of Doris screaming in my ear.

"We're late for the peace march, Mother." Tom and Doris led me back to the car. The traffic moved slowly on. I felt drowsy and even the sound of Doris and Tom shouting and arguing about getting to the peace rally didn't keep me awake.

When I finally woke up I was alone in the car, but I was surrounded by a crowd of noisy people. They all had banners, each one mentioning a different war. I wondered how long I'd been sleeping, and whether I'd missed a war. Doris and Tom finally pushed through the crowd and got in the car.

"We decided to let you sleep, Mum," Doris said kindly. "It was terrible anyway. They were all hitting one another with their banners. The dignitaries couldn't get out of the first two rows because of flying objects."

"Talking about flying objects," said Tom, as he wiped what looked like a squashed tomato from his lapel, "we thought you'd lost it a bit back there on the bridge. I suppose you knew what you were doing, I know we didn't. I saw the TV cameras. I just hope they don't name any names."

"Yes," said Doris, "let's get home and see it on TV."

"Oh, I don't want to see it on TV," I told them. "The movie was much better." They gave me a puzzled look as though they intended to ask a question. They shook their heads at one another and changed their minds.

Sept. 4th

This morning Doris and Tom drove me over to Fred, my youngest son, and Gerty his wife. As well as being parents to Sandy and Gillian, Fred and Gerty also take care of their grandson Rolly. Rolly's eight years old. His father is Fred and Gerty's son, Paul, who was married to Jane, but they died five years ago. They were missionaries and died in Africa. After that Rolly was shipped home to his grandparents where he gets lots of love and has settled down nicely. He adores Sandy. We had a really good breakfast; Sandy and Fred cooked sausages on their new barbecue. Gerty seems to have forgiven me for "stealing the limelight" as she puts it, at Gillian's wedding. Gerty wiped barbecue sauce from Rolly's chin and helped him into his jacket.

"Shirley's coming soon to take you for a walk," Gerty told Rolly. Shirley is the babysitter. She has an apartment not far from where Gerty and Fred live. Rolly likes Shirley a lot.

"Can I go to Shirley's apartment after a walk, Nanny?" Rolly asked Gerty. "She's got unicorns on the wall and a fish tank and she lets me jump up and down on her bed."

"I don't think you should jump on Shirley's bed," said Gerty.

"I didn't do it last time," he said.

"Good," said Gerty.

"There wasn't room…Pete was lying on it," said Rolly.

"Pete was on her bed?"

"Yes. He was waiting while she ironed his pants."

"What was he doing without his pants?" Gerty shouted. She was making sure that Fred heard. He was on the patio cleaning the barbecue. I like to sit back and hear the young ones interact. Gerty turned back to Rolly.

"So Rolly, you were going to tell me why he didn't have his pants on." Rolly shrugged his shoulders.

"Well, how can he wear them if she's ironing them?" I have to say that I thought it was a silly question too. The front door buzzer went just then. It was Shirley.

"Hello," said Gerty. Fred waved from the patio. "I want you to take Rolly for a nice walk in the park, Shirley," Gerty said. "Then bring him straight back here."

"You betcha, Mrs. Rayton," Shirley's always polite and easy to get along with.

"Now here's some money to give to the buskers if there are any in the park today." Gerty stuffed some quarters into Rolly's pocket. Fred keeps reminding me that Gerty is a patron of the arts. "Now," she went on, "tell him which ones are playing in tune, Shirley, we don't want to encourage any duds."

"You betcha," says Shirley. "Will do."

I fell asleep in the sun on the patio. I woke up in a cloud of smoke. Fred was cooking on the barbecue again. Sandy came back from a date, gave me a hug and then used his expertise with the barbecue to get rid of the smoke. The clouds rolled by and I realized I was hungry. Sandy put plates around the table.

"I've just seen our Rolly," Sandy told us. "He's singing in the park, by the concession stand." Gerty dropped the plate she was holding. Sandy, with a deft move, caught it in mid-air. He laughed.

"You should hear him. He's singing his little heart out."

"What's he singing?" I wanted to know.

"'Puff the Magic Dragon,'" said Sandy. Gerty turned to Fred who was humming a few bars of 'Puff.'

"Fred. Go get him immediately."

"Leave the kid alone," said Sandy. "He's having the time of his life. People are throwing money at him."

"Where on earth was Shirley?" Gerty asked. She put her hand to her chest as though she was having one of her indigestion attacks.

"Oh, she's there, everything's fine. You should see the people! Shirley's wearing that skirt, you know, that comes to here." He pointed to the top of his legs.

"The little hussy," said Gerty. "She must have gone home and changed." Sandy went on with his story.

"She's shaking a tambourine...among other things." Fred took off the apron with the caption 'I can take the heat.'

"I'd better go and see this."

"Yes, do go, Dad," said Sandy. "She's also wearing that sweater you like with 'Climb Every Mountain,' on it." Fred rushed into the hall just as the front door opened. Shirley and Rolly came in smiling and out of breath. Rolly ran over to me, his little face flushed. It was lucky I was sitting down because he flung himself at me. His eyes sparkled as he emptied his pockets into my lap.

"Look," he said, "we earned four dollars and eighty-five cents, me and Shirley."

"You're a regular little entrepreneur," I said.

"A what?" he asked.

"You're a clever lad," I told him. Even Gerty didn't seem to want to spoil his day. Everyone was hungry and all was forgiven as we enjoyed our supper. Sandy offered to walk Shirley home. Gerty called out as they went to the front door.

"Just keep your pants on, young man."

Sandy answered in a really posh voice,

"I beg your pardon, Mom, I'm terribly offended." I could hear him and Shirley giggling as they closed the door.

At bedtime I told Rolly a story about his mum and dad. He likes to hear about them, even though he doesn't remember much about them. I told him how they saved a whole village in Africa.

"They tackled a big gorilla called King Kong." I said. This left him with a look of wonder on his face. Actually his mum and dad died of typhus. The story I told him had some truth in it; after all it was an animal that was involved in their deaths. I think it was a flea.

Sept. 5th

Sandy drove me back to Honeystone Mansion this morning. When I arrived on the fourth floor with Sandy, Rhodena, my favourite care aide, gave me a big hug. Sandy asked where was his hug? Rhodena was quite hot and flustered by the time she walked us to my room. She then went for Henry and the Dolly

Sisters. She even brought Arthur Proctor. They made a little welcome back party in my room. Sandy stayed a while. It was good to see my old friends and I had lots to tell them. Later on, I looked in on Monster. He sleeps a lot. I'm often curious about him, I wonder if he ever talks in his sleep. I sat by his bedside and I told him about the police arresting me for embezzlement, or whatever they thought I was doing, and the boy on the bridge. I said,

"I deserve an Oscar for my performance in saving his life." I told him that he would love Boadicea. "She weighs about the same as you and Rolly would love to meet you. I know because he loves King Kong."

Some day Monster will speak, I know he will.

Sept. 20th

I realize I haven't made any entries in my diary for a few days. I have been busy though, busy telling everyone about my visit with the family. I got a bit bored after a while and made a few things up. If you lie though, you need a really good memory. I was a bit lost for words when Ms. McPherson asked me how I enjoyed the castles on the Rhine.

"How did you fit it all in, after all it was just four days" she pointed out.

Sometimes I hate that woman.

Sept 27th

I was coming home a bit late this evening after popping into the Elephant and Castle pub on Dunsmuir Street. I was happily walking along, singing a few bars of 'I've got a Luverly Bunch of Coconuts.' I got as far as Robson Street when some young man riding a skateboard comes whizzing from behind. He whips my purse right off my shoulder and goes gliding on. A nice couple helped me back to Honeystone.

Tanya and Clive, the evening staff, were very concerned about me. I felt pretty upset but I soon cheered up when Clive read out a Honeystone Mansion rule from the policy book. Apparently, the administration people have informed the cost clerk (my arch enemy Mr. Snerd) to always reimburse residents for things that have been stolen.

Tanya and Clive made a list of the contents of my purse. It wasn't a long list.

"Any money?" Clive asked.

"Not much, I spent it on a glass of stout." I went on to remind him that administration took most of my money. "They had the nerve to lock it in the safe," I grumbled.

"Well, Clover, you do buy a lot of strange stuff. You know we've still got that lawsuit on, the one about that Cherokee Warrior plane you saw advertised. Where did you think you were getting sixty thousand bucks from?"

"It wasn't my fault," I told him. "The ad distinctly said, 'For sale, a Cherokee Warrior.' I thought I was adopting an Indian." Tanya tapped with her pencil.

"Let's get back to the purse, shall we? What was in there?"

"There were some handkerchiefs and some antacid tablets, some sticky toffee that was stuck to the lining so I just left it there, and a picture of me on the Queen Mary." I thought a bit more. "Oh, yes, and some laxative pills in a Smarty box." Clive slapped the desk and laughed. Then he did one of his wonderful pirouettes from his ballet dancing years.

"You put those shiny brown laxative pills in a Smarty box?"

"Yes," I said, "the bottle was too big to put in my purse."

"Shit," said Clive, "I hope the bum likes candy."

October

Oct. 1st

My grandson Sandy called me today. It's always good to hear from him.

"I know you're feeling bad about the creative writing classes being cancelled," he said. "You were just on a roll too, Grandma." Sandy had taken my story home to read. He went on to tell me that he thought <u>Lust is a Many Splendoured Thing</u> was great.

"I'll work on it a bit, Grandma," he told me. "This should be out there for the world to read. I think you and me are coming from the same place."

"Yes," I agreed, "you've got my genes. I've passed my articulation on to you."

"Never mind," he replied. "I'll get inoculated." He's always joking. "I'll just add a bit to your story here and there," he went on. "You know, make it more realistic." So evidently he's 'polished it up' as he puts it. He's going to go personally and hand the story in to some magazine he's heard of downtown. It's called *Red Hot and Randy*. I told Sandy I hadn't seen or heard of this magazine.

"That's because the stores have to keep it on the top shelf of the magazine rack," he said. "You could never reach it, Grandma."

Oct. 5th

There was the regular monthly meeting today of the staff and residents of Honeystone Mansion. I usually don't go to these meetings; it's a waste of time. They never want to do the things I tell them they should do, like firing Lorylee, for one thing. Also I've told them they should penalize doctors every time they say things like, 'of course you're not sleeping well, you're old, here's a pill.' They asked me to leave one time when I suggested that when a doctor gives you more than nine pills a day–and a lot of them do–he should be made to take all the pills himself for a month. Then he can start wondering why he can't sleep and what's happened to his bowels and his stomach.

I told them the same things today.

"Clover," Ms. McPherson said, "I want you to look at Mr. Svenson here." Olag Svenson jerked himself to attention on hearing his name. "Mr. Svenson, I'll have you know, Clover, is alive simply because of the pills his doctor prescribes. Right Mr. Svenson?" Olag looked at Ms. McPherson with a puzzled frown before speaking.

"Yes, yes. I'm here." Olag looked around as though he wasn't quite sure.

"For your information, Clover, he takes...I think it's eleven... is it Olag? And you're still alive at ninety-two, aren't you?" Olag didn't seem to know whether this was a question or a statement. He went with the question.

"Yes, I'm...alive."

"Yes, I know all that," I told her. "But they also tell me he was a cross-country skiing champion up to three years ago."

"Well, we had to stop that, Clover. He kept spraining his ankle and needing lots of attention."

Ms. McPherson flipped the sheet in front of her. "Next on the agenda?" she snapped. It was Mr. Snerd's turn to read his monthly financial report. He always tries to justify his meanness by picking on people. He went on about how Monster should be sent away.

"He costs us extra money," he rattled on. "We have to keep replacing his mattress because he's so heavy. And also he doesn't look...good; he gives a bad impression. He should be with people like...himself." Then Snerd went on and on about Arthur Proctor costing a lot of money for psychiatry treatment. "He could be better treated elsewhere. All this is costing money."

I turned to look at the few residents who were attending the meeting. "Hands up who thinks Snerd should be fired because he's costing us a lot of aggravation."

Everyone's hand shot up. Ms. McPherson hit the table in front of her.

"We've had enough for today," she said. "And, Clover, I'd like a word with you alone." I told her she'd find me in my room drafting a letter to the board of governors.

Oct. 9th

Sandy called again today. He had been to see the people at *Red Hot and Randy.*

"I like the people who work on this magazine," he told me. "They're on my wavelength. I handed in your story, Grandma, and I told them you live in Honeystone Mansion. They want to see you. Is it okay?"

"Sure," I said. "Anytime."

Oct. 14th

I can tell that fall is here. The professional gardeners came today. Old Ernie manages to do the day-to-day stuff but not the big jobs. It was sad to watch in a way. They pulled out a lot of the annuals including the marigolds, which are my favourites. They left them in a heap by the side of the path and went for lunch. I had one of my really dependable brainwaves. I got two plastic garbage bags from the cleaner's trolley and filled the bags with used styrofoam cups from the bin by the coffee machine, then I went to find the Dolly Sisters.

"I've got a horticultural job for you both," I told them. They stopped feeding their two gerbils from a box of popcorn. They keep the gerbils in a hanging birdcage for some reason. One of the gerbils seemed to think it could fly; it teetered off the edge of the cage door. Fortunately, it fell into the popcorn box, which both the twins were holding. One of them got the gerbil out by its hind legs and put it back in the cage. It munched happily away at a large piece of popcorn held in its front paws.

"Did you say something about culture, Clover?" said one.

"Oh, anything cultural we'll do, Clover," said the other. I took them down to the garden. Ernie always takes off in a huff when the professional gardeners come in. It's a good thing in a way. Ernie is missing part of his left arm. He has a hook instead of a hand. He does amazing things in the garden with this hook. When he first saw the gardeners come in, he looked at them just like Captain Hook looked at Peter Pan and the lost boys. There was a bit of a skirmish and one of the gardeners got his apron torn. Ms. McPherson, who's scared of Ernie anyway, made sure after this event that the Handy Dart would come whenever the gardeners came. Ernie would be given five dollars and taken to the Legion.

I found Ernie's bench for the twins to sit on. Joe, the janitor, always willing to help a good cause, brought a card table for the twins. The three of us filled the plastic cups half full of soil. The tabletop was full. The Dolly Sisters sat down and waited for the next move. I carried marigolds plants over from the pile. We stuffed a marigold plant into each cup. By the time the gardeners had returned we had at least two dozen cups of marigolds. I had to admit that the plants looked a bit forlorn. Some of the flower heads dangled over the sides of the cups. They looked like frightened people on a crowded boat about to sink.

"Now," I said to the twins, "this is where the cultural part comes in." Their faces lit up. "It's Saturday," I told them, "and lots of visitors will be coming soon. You know that we need extra money for Christmas. I want you both, in your cultured wonderful manner, to sell these plants to the visitors for...fifty cents each." They nodded. The twins love visiting day, even though no one seems to come to see them. I tend to share my visitors with them. The truth of the matter is, I get rid of some of my boring visitors by inviting the twins to my room. Then I leave for the day.

The twins sat happily on the bench, a sea of yellow marigolds in front of them. I brought them a warm drink every hour or so. As the afternoon wore on, they needed extra sweaters and a blanket for their knees. It seemed whenever I saw them they were engaged in conversation with visitors. The table, I noticed, got emptier. They used no sales pitch tactics. The visitors seemed to realize that the only way to get past these two chattering ladies was to buy a plant. It was four thirty when I woke from a short nap and went to find them. They were in the foyer counting the money.

"We made sixteen dollars and fifty cents," they said in unison. Later, an amused member of the staff told me the twins drove the professional gardeners crazy with their constant gabbing. They gave the twins five dollars to go away.

Oct. 16th

I had the weirdest conversation today with a couple of young women who said they were from R.H.R. One of them, a blonde girl, was dressed in leather boots and leather skirt and she wore a leather shoelace round her hair. Her face was white as chalk but her lips were bright red and perfectly shaped into a cupid's bow. The second girl was weighted down with metal. Chains hung round her neck and belt. A fine two-inch chain hung from the side of her nose; it ended in a tiny cross. She had black hair that she had somehow trained to stand on end. You felt as though you'd draw blood if you patted her on the head. She held a small camera and clicked it around the room. Her metal bracelets jingled as she moved.

"R.H.R?" I asked. "Isn't that a blood group?" The blonde girl swept everything on my dresser to one side then hopped on top. She took out a pencil and pad from her leather handbag and turned to the other young woman.

"Are we a blood group? Is she funny or what?" She smiled at me. "No," she said, "we're from *Red Hot and Randy...* R.H R." She swung her legs and looked round the room.

"Oh, Sandy told me about you," I said.

"Hey! Is he outstanding or what?" She nodded to the other girl. "This is Cyn. I'm Fran. Okay Cyn, here we go." Cyn was busy with her camera. She leant out of my window and took a shot of the back alley.

"Way to go," she shouted down to some unknown person doing God knows what. Fran still sat on my dresser licking the end of her pencil.

"Let's get down to it, Clover," she said. "Now there seems to be quite a bit of blood in this story. I want to ask you a question..." she leaned forward pointing her pencil at me. "Tell me, do you have a blood fetish or something?"

"No," I told her, "in fact I'm a bit anaemic if anything." Fran glanced at Cyn who was now lying on the floor. She appeared to be taking a picture of a spider web on the ceiling. Fran went back to her questions.

"Okay. We'll tell you what we like about your story and we'll tell you what we'd like you to work on. We love the nude party in the hothouse."

"Nude party!" I was startled. "I seem to remember only Deedry took her clothes..."

"No, no," she interrupted looking down at the notebook on her knee. "We've got here Chrystal, Tiffany, Amber and a rock band all in the nude."

"Well...whatever," I said.

"About Aunt Skitsy," she went on. "Is Skitsy a dyke? It'll be much more interesting if she is." Fran looked hopefully at me.

"No…there's no dyke," I replied, "I think you're getting mixed up with the moat…You know…the moat that went round the castle?" The young woman shrugged.

"What about the bats?"

"Yes?"

"Was there some sex symbolism with the bats?"

"No, they were just your ordinary bloodsucking Dracula bats."

"Right…Now we liked the part where the priest is…" she referred to her notes again, "licking the banana pulp off Deedry's body…"

"Oh, did he lick it off? I don't remember that…"

"Now about the ending…"

"Yes?"

"We need a happy ending. Let's say Hades goes to Rome, right? He sees the Pope, right? Then, just as the Pope is handing him his…" She looked again at her notes. "…frock…someone in the crowd shoots him, right?"

"You call that a happy ending? Hades getting shot?"

"No, no, I mean the Pope."

"Oh, well…it has happened before," I said undecidedly. Fran leapt down from the dresser and came to sit beside me on the bed.

"You can do it. It'll be great. I can see it now." Cyn had stopped taking photos. She stood gazing at her friend.

"That's great, Fran," she said. "Then Hades can come back, shack up with Deedry again and we can serialize." They looked at me as though they had discovered the secret of the universe.

"Go for it, Clover," said Fran as she put her notebook and pencil in her purse. They were heading for the door, then Cyn decided to flip aside the curtain that divides me from Maisey. She held up the camera and clicked. As the light in the camera flashed, Maisey gave a frightened scream.

"Whoo," said Cyn. "The fat lady sings." She slung the camera over her shoulder. Fran opened the door and pointed a red-tipped finger at me.

"You are going to be fay-mus," she said.

"Well," I told her, "I'll hand it over to Sandy. I think he's the one for the job."

"Hey," said Fran, "is he outstanding or what? Just remember to tell him this. If it ain't randy, it ain't dandy." She beckoned to her friend "We're outta here, Cyn."

I stretched out on my bed quite exhausted. I could hear Maisey murmuring, "I'm blind, I'm blind."

"It's just temporary, Maisey," I told her. "Whereas my problems go on forever."

I closed my eyes. I'll have to speak to Sandy about the nude party and the dyke and the other stuff. I can't seem to remember it all. I had a long nap hoping it would come back, but it didn't.

Oct. 21st

I was dozing off last night when I heard noises. Someone was in the back alley just below my window. When I leaned out, I saw it was Snerdy Turdy. He'd just closed his car door and was whispering to a woman. The two of them could be clearly seen in the light of our back door lamp. All ninety-five pounds of Snerd was aquiver. The woman probably also weighed about ninety-five pounds, fifty of them in her chest.

"I'll just sneak in here through the back door and get my keys," Snerd said as he kissed the end of her nose.

"Silly Willy," she giggled shaking her mop of red curls, her long glass earrings glinting in the light.

"I know...I was stupid to leave the keys on my desk." This time he kissed her chin.

"Silly Billy." She leaned back on the hood of the car, opening her cloth coat as she did. I could practically hear Snerd panting from my window. "I'm coming with you, Clarence," she said. "I want to see where you take care of these...old...old...people." He bent over her and pursed his lips.

"My little coochy coo," he said bending lower and lower, his lips still puckered. He seemed to be aiming rather low I thought. I decided I'd seen enough mushy stuff for one night. Before his lips could land on their target I shouted down.

"Hey! You're waking everybody up with that racket down there." The woman gave a little shriek and clutched at Snerd who looked up and shook his fist.

"I might have known you'd be the only one awake at this hour," he hissed.

"No, I'm not."

"Yes–you–are." He jumped with each word. I leaned as far out of the window as I dared, then I looked up at the fifth and sixth floors above me. I shouted as loudly as I could.

"Is anybody else awake because of this din?" In a few seconds windows opened, angry voices could be heard.

"What's up? What's going on?"

"Is it another bloody fire drill?"

"Oh, look. It's Snerd."

I spoke in a normal voice to Snerd.

"There you are," I told him. "I may have to report you to Ms. McPherson."

Snerd's girl friend squealed. Snerd must have told her about our director. Snerdy Turdy pointed menacingly at me, I couldn't make out what he was spluttering about but the woman clapped her hands over her ears. I closed the window and went back to bed. I'd better stay out of Snerd's way for a day or two.

Oct. 25th

Today a TV crew stopped me. I was passing the fountain on Georgia Street. They had lights and cameras, and a small crowd had already gathered. An attractive young woman held the mike in front of me, wanting to know my reaction to some news item. Apparently boxing might be taken out of the Olympic Games. I had to wonder why they would ask an old lady. I decided to give my opinion. I took the mike from the young woman's hand. She didn't want to part with it but I managed to wrestle it from her.

"Why don't we ask some of the children standing here?" A couple of children waved at me. "Now in this athletic sport," I proceeded to tell them, "two men get into a ring. It's not really a ring because it's square. Anyway, they get into this square ring and hit one another till one of them is unconscious."

The young interviewer interrupted. "But there are rules, you know, in boxing."

"Yes, of course there are." I agreed. Two of the children standing near the front of the small crowd looked about ten. I addressed my words to them. "You mustn't hit anyone in the stomach, but you can hit them on the head as much as you want." The mother of the young children reached down and took their hands; she turned to pull them away. They weren't in a hurry to leave. A few people made comments, the interviewer tried to take the mike from me and an argument broke out. An old man told me I didn't know what I was talking about.

"Would you like me to unplug your ears with the mike?" I asked him.

He stepped closer. "Are you threatening me?"

The interviewer reached over and tried again to take the mike. We scuffled a bit, this time she won.

"That's right, take the bloody thing off her," the old man said. The young man holding a bright light said something about free speech. The old man put up his fists, he was weaving quite badly as he tottered toward the young man. I could see trouble approaching. I don't like violence so slipped away. I went off to the Army and Navy store. I'd promised to pick up some Hulk Hogan wrestling videos for Arthur Proctor.

Oct. 26th.

I'm glad I'm getting my bearings and finding my way to all my old haunts. I even find my way back to Honeystone Mansion most of the time. I like having my lunch now and then at the community college on Dunsmuir. It's one of the cheapest places in town. I was there today. I was sitting down to enjoy my Eccles cake and tea, when a well-dressed man of about seventy sat down next to me. He took off his raincoat and hat, tugged at his fancy waistcoat, straightened his tie and then put his umbrella beside mine at the end of the table. I couldn't help comparing it with my own. His was black and sleek. It had a silver tip at one end and a curved polished wooden handle at the other. My poor battered umbrella had three ribs coming away from the fabric. I'd lost the handle God knows where. The colour of mine was dirty beige, with rusty overtones.

"So," he asked, "do you live in these parts?"

"Yes," I answered, "I live in a home for the elderly just off Robson Street."

"I wouldn't be found dead in a place like that," he snapped.

"Oh," I replied, "we're often found dead." He stuffed a quarter of the danish pastry into his mouth and sniffed.

"I bet half of you didn't eat right when you were younger, that's why you're there."

"I don't know...I used to eat quite well..."

"Nuts."

"I beg your pardon?" I said,

"You should be eating a lot of nuts. I practically live on them." He popped a bit more pastry into his mouth. I had been trying to think what he reminded me of. It dawned on me. He was like a squirrel, an angry squirrel that had forgotten where it had put its acorns.

"And another thing," he was off again. "You could have had private care if you'd looked after your money."

"Taking care of my money wasn't the problem," I told him. "Getting some money to take care of was..." He didn't wait for me to finish.

"Although I have to admit," he confessed, "I did lose some money when I put it into shady debentures once."

"Oh, I didn't lose mine," I chirped. "I put it in an old sock."

"I bet half of you can't see properly either." I knew more was coming so I waited while he finished another mouthful of Danish. "You should be eating carrots for your eyes. I don't miss much I can tell you."

"Well," I said, "I do miss a few things I suppose, but I can't help noticing the big blob of jam that's just fallen off your danish onto your tie." He was quiet for a moment while he cleaned himself up.

"I'll get special attention when I need it," he was off again. "First class all the way, none of this waiting for buses and free handouts for me." He stuffed the last of his food into his mouth, finished his tea and waved the cup at me. "I stand in line for no one," he firmly announced.

"I see. Who lined up for your danish then?" He ignored this.

"And then there's brain food you know...that means fish," he volunteered.

"They give us fish every Friday," I told him. He wasn't interested.

"I have brains I've never even used," he told me.

"I have brains, too," I said, "but they're all working full tilt." He stood and put on his coat. He wagged his finger at the remains of my Eccles cake.

"Your memory and your brains are important," he said as he fastened the top button of his raincoat. He seemed to be under the impression that I was going to have my memory and my brains removed. "Quick," he snapped, "what day is it?"

"Er..." I was taken off guard.

"There you see. You don't know." He put his hat on his head, said "Good day," and left, leaving his umbrella.

I sat a while sipping my tea and wondering what day it really was. Then I remembered. It was Monday. If I got back by two o'clock I'd see the second half of *Gone with the Wind* on our giant TV screen. I put on my coat and picked up the two umbrellas. I walked over to the young man taking the money at the counter.

"A man will be coming back to ask for his umbrella," I told him. "Give him this..." I hummed "Singing in the Rain" as I walked back to Honeystone Mansion, covered by the sleek black umbrella with the polished wooden handle and a silver tip at the end.

Oct. 31st

It's Halloween already. The Activity Department is going to have a dressup party. Henry's going to be a wolf and I'm going to be Red Riding Hood. I heard the Dolly Sisters say that they were looking for wigs. They're both going to the party as Shirley Temple.

"I think I know where we can all get wigs," I told them. "There's a row of shops on Granville Street where they sell funny stuff. Let's go."

We set off along Robson Street. We got the usual gawks from people. You'd think no one had ever seen identical twins before. The Dolly Sisters were both talking to people at the same time, but they usually say the same thing, so it's alright. While I was waiting for them to catch up, I did what I usually do. I popped in and out of the stores along the way. I just asked quick questions to keep the clerks on their toes. I called from the doorway of Elite, the exclusive shoe shop...

"How much are the black shoes in the window, the ones with the steel tips and six inch heels?"

"Four hundred and seventy-five dollars, Madam," the girl replied.

"Do you have a pair in purple?" I asked. I'd gone before she came back with the answer.

From the doorway of the little watch shop I asked, "What is the correct time please?" The man looked up from the watch he was fixing.

"Um..." He looked along the row of watches on the counter and then at all the clocks on the wall. They were all at slightly different times.

"I would like the absolute proper time," I told him. He looked down at the watch on his wrist, smiled at me and opened his mouth. "Forget it," I said as I dashed for the door. I had seen the Dolly Sisters go by. I caught up to them just as a fancy sports car stopped at the curb. The occupants seemed to be very amused about something. The driver shouted to us so we walked over.

"Can I ask you a couple of questions, Grandma?" asked the young man who was driving. He looked around at the passengers and grinned, and then he looked back at me. "Where do you buy your clothes? And where's the Pan Pacific hotel?"

"We send away to the third world for our clothes." I told him. "Now... to get to the Pan Pacific, go down there," I pointed back where we had come from, "and make a left on Bute Street and it's on the first corner." They sped off while I was still leaning on the car. The Dolly Sisters managed to catch me.

"Clover! Why did you send them to Honeystone Mansion?" one of the sisters asked.

"Yes, you sent them to Honeystone," said the other.

"Well, if it's good enough for us, it's good enough for them," I told her.

Just before we turned onto Granville Street, we put five cents each in the hat of the old man playing his flute on the corner. It's worth five cents because we get to sing along for a while. We sang "The Hills are Alive with the Sound of Music," and "My Way." The man stopped playing like he always does.

"Do you want your money back?" he asked. We know this is a hint for us to go. Some people can't stand competition.

We finally got onto Granville Street and stopped at a dingy little shop. Between all the crosses painted on the window we could see Halloween masks and a mannequin wearing a swim-suit. It had holes in the weirdest places. When we walked into the shop it was strange because everybody else walked out. The man behind the counter looked surprised and even a little scared when he saw us.

"Ladies," he said, "I want you to know, I run a very clean establishment."

"Oh, I don't know about that," said one of the Dolly Sisters. She was running her white-gloved finger along a row of rubber penises attached to the wall. She held up her dusty finger for him to see. "These look very dirty to me." The other sister had gone over to the far wall; she was peering through a little hole. Then I remembered why we were there.

"Do you have false hair?" I asked the man behind the counter. I seemed to catch him off guard.

"No, no," he said, clapping his hand on top of his head.

"All right, all right," I answered, "that's all I want to know." I called to the sisters.

"Come on, we'll have to try somewhere else."

"Wait a minute. Wait a minute." It was the twin at the peep-hole. "Someone is moving in here." The other sister was now dusting some whips.

"Come on," I told them. "I'm going."

"I do wish you'd both come and see this," the sister at the peephole pleaded, "It's very educational." I headed for the door; the twins followed, tut-tutting all the way.

As I reached for the door handle, the three of us stopped in amazement. We hadn't noticed as we came in, but hanging to one side of the door was a large balloon. It was the life size figure of a nude woman.

"Isn't that fascinating?" said one of the sisters.

"Isn't that fabulous?" said the other.

"She's a bit out of proportion," I said looking at her chest. As we moved to go, the sister who seemed to like dusting things, reached out with her gloved finger to the nude woman's grimy navel. Her purse slipped down her arm on to the floor right in front of me. I tripped on it and clutched at the nude woman's chest for support. She exploded with a bang. I turned to apologize to the man just in time to see him duck below the counter; it was as though he thought he'd been shot at.

A crowd gathered in the doorway. Me and the sisters were holding on to each other. Everyone shouted at once.

"Who got shot?"

"Are you all right?"

"Quick. Someone call a cop."

"Which one of you got shot?"

"No one," I answered. I pointed to the floor. "It's just this woman here—she exploded!" They all gathered round and stared at the bits of pink rubber on the floor.

The police came and drove us back to Honeystone Mansion. I felt nice and drowsy in the back of the car. I was vaguely aware of one of the policemen going on about how three nice old ladies like us should not be subjected to the depravity that goes on in some of the stores on Granville Street. I was almost sorry when we arrived back at Honeystone Mansion. The policemen helped us out of the car graciously.

"Thanks," I said. "We must hurry along; we have to get to the arts and craft department before they close. We're going to steal some wool and make some wigs."

November

Nov. 1st

I'm getting to the end of my funeral stuff. If any new people arrive I'll ask for some more forms and I'll endeavour to meet the newcomers on the first day of arrival in their rooms. I will say to them… "Welcome, what are your funeral arrangements?" Yes, I'll get them while their minds are still clear. No more waxworks and double coffins. These new people will be like me, they will have clear and sensible notions on the correct way to be disposed of. What happened to just plain getting buried in a hole, or the present day tendency of putting your loved ones in an incinerator? I've learned a lot of things about people. I know I didn't meet any of our old folk who seemed afraid to talk about dying. Sometimes, the staff get silly about it though. Yes, life moves us on, and death moves us off, as you might say.

Nov. 2nd

Ken Selacar died this morning. I had gone in to see him with a funeral form. There he was in front of his TV. The man on the game show was saying, "And the next category will be history." Well, that's what Ken Selacar is now. I rang his bell. Rhodena, my favourite care aide, and Judy, the nurse, came. They talked in whispers and tiptoed as though they might wake him. After they closed the drapes they switched off the TV.

"Hey! Leave it on," I said. "I was just trying to answer a question about what was bad about Ivan the Terrible?"

"Do you mind, Clover?" Judy shouted and then as though remembering something she whispered, "There's a dead man here, you know."

"I know," I answered, "I'm here on legitimate business. I came to give him a funeral form."

"Well, you're too late, aren't you?" Judy snapped as she guided me through the door.

When I got back to my room I filled out the funeral form myself. I happen to know that Ken wanted to be cremated. He also told me that he wanted his ashes sprinkled over the carpet in the main lounge of the Regency Tower Hotel. I think they asked him to leave one time over something to do with his sexual orientation. He didn't look Chinese to me, but I believe that people's last wishes should be obeyed. I'll have to get the Dolly Sisters to come along. We'll share the ashes between us. I've seen the carpet—it's a great big huge thing.

Nov. 7th

I sometimes look at the parcels left at the front desk. If the parcel is for someone I like, I offer to take it to them. Today there was a parcel addressed too, 'The Family of Ken Selacar c/o Honeystone Mansion.' The parcel was just a bit smaller than a shoebox. I lifted it and was surprised at how heavy it was. I know Ken had no family. Just a very well-dressed gentleman used to visit him. I was about to say something to Diane, who was busy on the phone. I looked again at the parcel and noticed the address in the top corner. It was the Serenity Funeral Parlour. I knew then that these were Ken's ashes. I quietly picked up the box and took it to my room.

Nov. 8th

The first thing I did this morning was open the box of ashes. I shared it into three lots and put each portion into a Kentucky Fried Chicken box. They were left over when me and Henry and Monster had eaten the chicken for a late snack. We are so sick of Lorylee's cooking. Thank goodness Sidney, the proper cook, is coming back from jail next week. He sent us a card—he's trying to get time off for good behaviour. He also said, 'I won't commit bigamy any more. I'll just love 'em and leave 'em from now on.' So I'm thinking of having a goodbye party for Lorylee. I happen to know that Arthur Proctor has made an interesting wall hanging out of the liver she's cooked since she's been here. Arthur's work of art is the size of a large dinner plate. He uses it as a dartboard. The administration wants it out of the room. They insist it's a health hazard. I admit it has turned green and does smell a bit. Lorylee might as well take it with her. I'll also gift wrap two dozen of her hard boiled eggs. We've been painting them in the hobby room.

Nov. 9th

We had a special meeting today to decide what we will do for our Remembrance Day ceremony. I was very proud of Henry. They asked him to play the "Last Post" on his trumpet. Then Verna the activity aide asked us,

"Can anyone speak French?" No one answered. "We would like someone to sing the national anthem in French." Verna looked around hopefully. "The Dolly Sisters will do their usual duet in English," she told us. I could see the twins squirming with delight. I wanted to choke them. I got thinking I've learned a lot of bits of French over the years. I've read it on cereal boxes and stuff at the supermarket. I even went to France once when the Queen Mary, which I was sailing on, picked some people up there on the way to Canada. Verna didn't ask for accuracy, she just asked for the anthem to be sung in French and I wanted to be part of things, like the Dolly Sisters and Henry. I put up my hand.

"I can do that," I told her. "You just want it sung in French, right?" I could see Verna was really pleased.

Before the meeting broke up, Verna asked Henry politely not to practice his trumpet on the balcony like he had been doing. "We've had complaints," she told him, "apparently they can hear you at St. Paul's Hospital." She suggested he practice downstairs in the locker room. That's fine because the acoustics are good down there. It's where Mr. MacTavish plays his bagpipes.

Nov. 11th

It was a lovely Remembrance Day ceremony. Arthur Proctor walked a little bit lopsided because all his medals were on the left side of his chest. Monster carried a huge flag; it scraped the ceiling in a few places because he's so tall. I noticed Snerd looked at the ceiling then covered his eyes with one hand. Later, he furiously scribbled something in the notebook he always carries with him. At least four clergymen were there covering all the religious denominations. I'm sure the only thing left out was Voodoo. For an altar we had a TV tray covered with a crotchet doily from arts and crafts. Two professional young men played the piano and the violin. All the clocks were wrong so we had to guess when it was time for the two minutes silence. Henry was super; nearly every note was on target. The Dolly Sisters sang the anthem in English, a bit weak I thought. Then I was asked up to the mike. Every bit of French I'd ever known came to my aid. I sang with a lot of feeling.

"Mercy bow coo. Garson lay parley voo.
Fem aye lar port. Oh dee cologne lamour.
Jer voo sem bow coo. Portage on tray new.
Shawn say leeze aye, none dee plume.

Cordon blue fro marge. Parree bon voy arge.
Mon dew, arret aye, un, der, twar.
Jer swee fransay. Jer swee anglay.
Soo flay mon shumy, boot on ear, wal are.
Mode dee employ, booje war, wee ooh lar lar."

It was very quiet when I finished. I could tell they were moved; stunned even. Verna's eyes were closed. Someone was fanning her with the doily from the altar. The young man on the piano was making strange noises behind a big white handkerchief. I think he was crying.

Nov. 14th

The Dolly Sisters and I did the special ceremony of the scattering of the ashes of Ken Selacar today; he can now rest in peace. We went over to the Regency Towers Hotel. I gave the twins a Kentucky Fried Chicken box of ashes each. The lobby wasn't too crowded so we had elbowroom. The carpet, where the ceremony was to take place, nearly fills the lobby. In the centre of the carpet there is a huge peacock. Its tail fans out and the colours are spectacular.

"Concentrate on the bird," I advised the Dolly Sisters. "We have to make the ashes last." We opened the tops of our boxes and proceeded. As we moved around we sang a few bars of "Let It Be." A young man in uniform came out of the elevator and stood watching.

"Are you the carpet cleaners?" he asked. We ignored him. This was sacred work we were doing. The young man persisted.

"Is this a new way of doing it or something?" His attention was taken up then by an old couple. They skirted the edge of the carpet sneezing all the way to the elevator. All the time we were performing this religious task, a young boy who looked about seventeen kept wheeling a luggage cart through. He stared at us all the way, but went carefully round the edge of the carpet. He was always followed by guests and the larger people had to walk sideways in some places. All this time the receptionist was leaning over her desk at the far side, watching with interest. We had now almost covered the peacock; it looked like a very unattractive pigeon.

Suddenly, a tall stout older man in a tuxedo came out of the elevator. If he'd been a bottle he would be just about to pop his cork.

"What the Hell!" he shouted at the young man. "What are you letting them do this for, Keith?" Keith raised both arms and shrugged.

"I thought you'd sent for them, sir." I almost expected him to salute. The older man's face looked a bit like Arthur Proctor's liver display. While Tux and Keith had a shouting match we, with reverence, shook the last of the ashes from our boxes with a flourish. Even we started to sneeze and laugh. I noticed a little of the ash had stuck to some of the chicken grease, but the rest was well used. The Dolly Sisters put their hands together and said "Amen, amen," and we headed for the door.

"Just a minute," shouted the older man. "You're going to have to pay for this...devastation. Keith!" he shouted. "Do something, quick!"

"Shall I get the dust-buster then?" Keith asked.

"I'll bust you in a minute," the big man barked. Then he noticed there was a small audience of guests standing around. He smiled at them sheepishly. They seemed too interested to leave as they looked back and forth from the men to us. They appeared to be waiting for the next act. Since the Dolly Sisters and I love to sing, this seemed to be a good opportunity for us. I looked into the faces of our eager visitors.

"Please join us in a tribute to our lost friend." While we walked slowly around the murky peacock on the edge of the carpet, we did our rendering of "To Dream the Impossible Dream." A few of the guests covered their faces. I think it was the dust. No one paid attention to the man in the tuxedo waving his arms. Maybe they thought he was our conductor. Then, as we were trilling on the last words of our song, he spoiled the mood.

"You will be sued for this. Mark my words."

The crowd looked puzzled. I don't think they thought our singing was that bad. Old Tux's cheeks puffed. I could see his blood vessels struggling to erupt. Keith had disappeared. The young luggage wheeler came through the door just then. With a resigned expression, he wheeled his cart right through the peacock, leaving four wheel tracks. Now you could have played noughts and crosses on it. I pulled myself to my full height, which I think is about five foot one and a half.

"Kindly address your remarks to this person," I said as I placed a card on the dusty, but lovely, Queen Anne table. The card read...'Mr. Snerd, Cost Clerk, Honeystone Mansion.' The three of us put our Kentucky Fried Chicken boxes beside the card and moved to the door. We could hear a commotion behind us, I turned. Tux was trying to get through the crowd which was now milling around the peacock's head. His bloodshot eyes were fixed on the three of us. Luckily he tripped over a guest's Pekinese dog, which had stopped to pee in the ashes. Now the peacock looked like a badly abused pigeon. The twins and I squashed together into the same section of the circulating door. We whizzed around twice, then shot out and headed for a number five bus.

Nov. 20th

It was a lovely fall day today. Me and Henry had seen the message on the bulletin board, which said that a bus would be arriving to take a small group of us bird watching in Stanley Park. I alerted the gang on the fourth floor. Arthur Proctor, of course, pretended to misunderstand what bird watching meant.

"Have these birds got two legs?" he asked. "And chests out here?" He held his hands about two feet from his body.

"Yes," I told him. He had his coat on in no time. The Dolly Sisters grabbed their binoculars, and Nettie Spooner brought along some of her cookies. They tend to make you feel you're flying when you've eaten them, so it seemed appropriate. I insisted on taking Monster along because, as I explained, he never talks, but maybe with birds around he'd start whistling.

"It works for me," said Arthur Proctor.

At ten am, a very nice young man met us at the bus and told us he was a student from the university.

"I'm studying ornithology," he said.

"You'll know all about getting orny then?" said Arthur Proctor. I gave him a dig in the ribs. The young man went on brightly.

"My name is Benjamin. I know we will have a fun-filled and enlightening day."

"Right, lead the way, Benji," I told him.

When we arrived at the park he led us on a lovely secluded trail. Benji got a bit disconcerted now and then. Henry's artificial leg seemed to creak every time the young man saw something interesting.

"You just frightened away a red winged blackbird," he said a bit peevishly. We worked our way slowly to a small lake.

"This is Beaver Lake," whispered Benji as though he had just discovered the source of the Nile.

"Ooh, lovely," said one of the Dolly Sisters. "We love beavers, don't we, Felicia?"

"Yes, yes, Celicia, where're the beavers?" said the other.

"I used to have a hat made of a beaver," volunteered Arthur Proctor. "Maybe I should have brought a gun."

"We're here to watch birds," said Benji firmly. "Look, quick everybody! There's a red shafted flicker." Arthur Proctor, who had grumbled nearly the whole time, muttered...

"We're the ones who've been shafted. And I'm sick of all the twittering birds, and the honking of those big suckers floating on the water." Benji was busy looking through his binoculars. Arthur went on. "I wanted to go to the beach. I heard there was a nude beach somewhere."

"Shush... shush...I hear something," said Benji. We gazed in the direction of his pointing finger. Suddenly, a man appeared from between the trees. He was holding what looked like a child's bow; he had a couple of arrows sticking out of his belt. In the other hand he was holding a dead duck. He looked very scared and the reason was clear. None of us had noticed that Monster had disappeared, and here he was now close behind the man with the duck. Seven foot tall Monster was pointing at the dead duck, tears streaming down his face. The man with the bow and arrows was shaking.

"Tell him to back off or I'll shoot," the man said. He didn't seem to me to be in any condition to fire straight. Benji was pointing at the dead duck and screaming.

"What have you done? These are God's creatures!" The man looked around at Monster, then back at us. He knew he was outnumbered. He dropped the duck and quick as lightning disappeared through the trees. The Dolly Sisters called after him.

"Did you see any beavers?"

"Where are all the beavers?"

Benji was leaning on a tree. He now looked as though he'd again found the source of the Nile, but his best friend had fallen in and drowned. We gave him a couple of minutes to recover. Me and Henry watched with interest as Monster lumbered over to the dead duck. He stooped and picked it up, opened his jacket and put the bird close to his chest then fastened the jacket over the top.

"We'll get it back from him later," I whispered to Henry. "I may even have it stuffed and put it on his dresser. I can always send the bill to Snerdy Turdy."

"What a nice kind thing to do," said Henry. After a few minutes Benji seemed to recover.

"We must find the warden and notify him of this terrible thing."

"Yes," said Arthur Proctor, "and ask him where the nude beach is." Benji decided to take us all back to Honeystone Mansion and phone the park from there. On our way to the small bus he was sure he heard the song of a meadow lark. We all agreed, whatever it was, it was quite thrilling. At our age we know when young people need cheering up.

Nov. 21st

I got the dead duck out of Monster's room. I pretended I was going to ask Dr. Harrison to revive it with artificial resuscitation. Monster looked confused but he handed it over. I put it in a canvas bag that my oldest son gave me a few years ago. The bag had a picture of Princess Diana and Prince Charles on the side; it was made to commemorate their wedding. It seemed somehow appropriate to use it for a dead duck. I took it down to Snerd's office. He was very snotty when I asked him to have it stuffed.

"I don't give a hoot for all the ducks in the park. There're too many anyway," he said. I told him I would report him to the Parks Board and the Society for the Prevention of Cruelty to Animals as I stomped away with the dead duck.

Nov. 22nd

I'm tired of looking at this dead duck. I thought to myself, there must be a lot of hungry people in the world who would be glad of this. Then I remembered the old man who sits on our bench at the front door every day. His name's Willie. He doesn't seem to have a home. I once offered to use my influence and get him into Honeystone Mansion.

"No, no, no, I like the outdoors," he said, jiggling the two plastic garbage bags he always seems to have with him. "These are all my possessions," he told me. I went down to the front of the building to find him. I had to wait for a while but finally he came. He was quite pleased when I offered him the dead duck. I was a bit disappointed though when he said, "I'll get five dollars for this in Chinatown." I had visions of him cooking it over a spit on the beach with all his hobo friends. I let him keep the canvas bag too. I feel a bit sad every time I look at it anyway.

Nov. 23rd

I've delivered a funeral form to nearly everyone on the fourth floor. I have just had an exhausting discussion with Myra Bernstien. She's very deaf. Most people write down what they have to say to her. I can't be bothered so I just shout at the top of my lungs and there's usually a crowd at the door when I've finished. Today I took her a form and asked her what she'd like us to do when she dies. After a while, everyone on the fourth floor heard me tell her that her son Isaac could not climb up The Matterhorn and scatter her ashes.

"Your son, Myra, is seventy-five, you are ninety-six. You'll be lucky if you don't have to climb a mountain with his ashes." She pointed to a certificate on the wall. "Yes, I know he finished dental school, Myra," I said. "But he retired from dentistry twenty years ago." She looked a bit puzzled. I cheered her up by reminding her that he comes from Florida every six months to see her.

"Who?" she asked.

"Never mind, just sign here," I told her. "I'll put your name down for the Serenity Place where I'm going." I couldn't help thinking Serenity should be giving me a discount; I've given them quite a bit of business.

Nov. 24th

I have always been a civic-minded person. Today I read the *Westender*, which is a free newspaper; it's delivered here each week. They leave about six copies and there are at least ninety-six of us living here. I go down early, take all six and distribute them to the few people who are like me, thinking straight, have an opinion about things, and know what's best for other people. I read that there was a town-planning event at Robson Square. I think they need wise old people like me to tell them what they are doing wrong with our city, and how they can put it right.

I looked around for my group of friends, the few 'with it' people who backed me up at the meeting on Yearly Summer Events when I said that the Indy 500 should be run along Robson Street, and through Stanley Park, so we could watch it from the roof of our building. But today, I found no one to share my enthusiasm. Henry was involved with a game of carpet bowling with Arthur Proctor. Monster had been taken for a walk by one of the volunteers, and I could hear Nettie Spooner playing the organ and singing "The Hallelujah Chorus." This is always a sign that that she's been eating her special cookies and she's high as a kite. I was stuck with the Dolly Sisters.

Quite a few people were at Robson Square for the event. There were even TV people filming everything.

"Now look interested," I said to the twins, "and ask intelligent questions."

"Yes, Clover," they said. We wandered around some very interesting exhibits. A bunch of university students asked us questions about improving our lives and said they would write up any plan we suggested and send it to city hall. They showed quite a bit of enthusiasm when I explained that we had a flat roof on the top of our building; I pointed out how easily a helicopter could land there.

"You know," I told them, "it would be much more satisfactory than riding round the city in that old bus of ours." I also suggested weekly sing-a-longs for seniors at the stadium.

A miniature reproduction of the west end of the city was the highlight of the town planning show. Two young men in smart business suits presided over the replica, which was set up on a stand about the size of a ping-pong table.

"How do you like the plan of our future fair city?" one of the men asked. "We're hoping for some input by the local community," he continued. He glanced at the camera as he spoke. It was turned in our direction. We came nearer to the table.

"Ooh, look at the doll houses," said one of the twins.

"And the little doll people," said the other.

"Well, I'd pull this down," I told the young man. I was pointing to a very tall office building. "And that, and that," I said, indicating a couple more tall buildings. I couldn't loosen any of the tiny models with my hands; I had to settle for pushing them with my umbrella. "Where are all the little parks for us to sit when we're tired of shopping?" I asked.

"We can't tear all the buildings down," he said. "You see, Madam, that particular one that you just knocked over with your umbrella is twenty-two storeys high and already exists." He smiled quickly at the camera then back at me.

"Well," I told him. "You should have asked me before you built it."

"Progress has to take place, Madam," he said. I looked closely at all the buildings and managed to find Honeystone Mansion. I looked for the park where I watch the pigeons. Fortunately I found it.

"Don't dare touch that," I said. "It's hallowed ground."

"There are some...um...future ideas...um, for parks...incorporated in the plan." The young man seemed to be addressing the camera, not me.

"You don't sit in parks very often do you?" I asked him. The man looked at me as though he would rather have been in a park at that moment. He glanced over at his friend who was in charge of the other end of the model. His partner was occupied. He was listening to the Dolly Sisters twittering about something.

"Where're the washrooms?" one of the twins asked.

"Yes, where are the washrooms?" said the other. The young man looked down at them. He smoothed back his thick blonde hair then obligingly pointed to spots around the board. He smiled at the camera and then, as though giving important information to the whole world, said, "You will find toilet facilities in various parts of the city, for instance...here and here, and,...yes, here and here." He smiled at the twins. They looked vacantly back at him.

"Yes, but where are the washrooms?"

"Where are they?" the twins looked appealingly at the young man. He became a bit cross. He tugged at his tie; he had forgotten the camera now.

"I've just told you ladies, the washrooms are all over the place," he swept his arm over the table. "There, there, there, and there." The Dolly Sisters looked as though they were about to cry. My young man was also in a snit. He was trying unsuccessfully to stand up the building I had knocked down.

The Dolly Sisters were looking imploringly at their angry young man.

"We only want to pee."

"Yes, we just want to pee." He exchanged a look of relief with his friend. The two of them lifted their arms in unison pointing to a door at the back of the room. The camera panned over to the sign which said Public Washrooms. The cameras followed the three of us as we sashayed toward the sign. It seemed a good time to leave.

Nov. 25th

On the bulletin board today there was a poster, each word done in different colours. It was really eyecatching. It said that over the next few days there would be four creative painting lessons. I think that after four lessons I could probably become quite an accomplished painter. Some things come naturally to me. The sign also said 'At the end of the lessons an art critic will judge your work. The best of the paintings will be put up in the quiet room for a month.' According to the sign, all the paints and canvases are free. Me and Henry will give it some serious thought.

Nov. 26th

Me and Henry decided that as it was raining we would go to the first art class today. A beautiful young woman met us at the activity room door. She was our teacher. Her name 'Celina,' was written in red, across the top of her black silk smock. She wore a lovely scarf around her dark hair. The scarf hung past her waist and was covered with chrysanthemums and roses. Long gold earrings hung to her shoulders.

"Sit, sit," she sang. We found ourselves places at the big oblong activity table. In front of each of us was a piece of construction paper. Each paper was about two foot square. There was also a brand new paintbrush, a jar of clean water and some saucers of paint. It looked as though this could be fun. I was reminded of being a child again, of coming home from school and showing my art work to my parents. They would look at each other strangely; I guess they were awestruck, just as they were with most of my schoolwork and report cards.

Looking around I counted ten people. Only half of us were from the fourth floor. It surprised me and Henry to see Arthur Proctor there.

"I took one look at this chick," Arthur said, pointing to the young teacher, "and decided that whatever she's teaching I'm going to learn, even if it's Greek." I looked at the back of the class. Nettie was there. She looked, I think they call it, 'spaced out.'

Henry said, "She's obviously under the influence of her funny cookies."

"I'm dying to see what she paints," I told him.

I like our fourth floor to be well represented and I realized the Dolly Sisters were missing. I had seen them earlier sitting in the foyer watching the rain. I raised my hand and told Celina that I had two more customers for her. I went and got them, and pushed the sisters into the room. They spent quite a while jabbering about where they were going to sit.

"Sit, sit," the teacher ordered them. The twins immediately sat down on one chair. Someone fetched them another chair and Celina brought extra paper and brushes, then she waved her arms.

"Paint, paint," she trilled. Standing beside Celina was a large piece of cardboard on an easel. As though to show us what she meant, she picked up a brush, dipped it in the dish of red paint sitting in front of Arthur Proctor and then slashed it across her paper. We all gasped. It seemed as though she'd ruined a nice clean sheet. She laughed and did the same thing again a little lower down. She then did some wiggly lines and finished with a big dot in the top right corner. She dropped the brush onto the ledge of her easel.

"Be brave, be brave," she chanted. I picked up my brush and dipped it into the green paint and made a sweeping movement with it. Unfortunately I went too far and covered a couple of inches of Henry's sheet.

"It's okay," he whispered, "I was going to put some grass there anyway." We all quietly got to work. The Dolly Sisters bent their heads. They did their painting in unison. If one put a stroke on her page, the other did exactly the same. They must be painting the same thing I thought to myself. I hope they meet in the middle.

It seemed as though I had hardly done anything before Celina called out,

"Time's up, time's up." She walked around picking up our paintings and setting them on a long shelf. As her arm floated passed me, I could see Nellie's picture; it looked like a drunken angel sitting on a cloud. Celina gaily waved us all through the door.

Nov. 27th

Even though it was a sunny day, me and Henry went to the art class. Celina pointed to the pile of our paintings.

"Find it, find it," she sang. Everyone was soon busy painting. I decided I would use every colour of paint there was. I would go surrealistic. We quietly worked while the teacher walked circles around us. She hummed and patted our shoulders. I liked Celina because she never criticized. She stopped behind Henry for a while, he was painting a horse. She tapped his shoulder.

"Clop, clop," she said laughing. Henry looked pleased. She danced to the side of Arthur Proctor who was in front of me. I looked over to see what he was doing. He had almost finished a painting of a nude woman. He was having some difficulty with her knees. I noticed the woman in his picture happened to be wearing long earrings and a scarf round her hair. Celine stopped and placed her first finger on the navel of Arthur's nude woman. It seemed to cause her to break her pattern of repeating everything twice.

"You have conceived a rare conceptualization of…" she clutched her throat, "quintessence," she murmured. Arthur looked down at his painting and back at Celina.

"I've conceived what?" he asked.

"Keep it up, keep it up," she warbled as she moved on. Arthur looked over at Henry.

"It ain't easy to keep it up at my age." Henry didn't look up; he was busy putting a mane on his galloping horse. I made a point of peeking over Nettie's shoulder. The angel was now holding a ukulele. She also held a bunch of balloons.

"I like those coloured balloon," I told her.

"Silly," she said. "They're brain cells."

Nov. 28th

We were reminded today that tomorrow would be the last art class session. Tomorrow would be the judging. I added some more colours to my painting. I filled in every spare space. I glanced at Henry's painting. It looked great. Even Arthur's nude woman had real kneecaps now. I wasn't very happy about my own picture and time was running out. People were working at a fever pitch. I watched as Nettie Spooner held up her painting and waved it in the air.

"That's a really good rain cloud," I remarked, I was looking at a dark shape next to the brain cells.

"It's a pancreas, my dear," she said in a far off voice.

"Sorry," I said. "And how about those dots, what are they?"

"Silly, that's undigested food." She stood and wobbled a bit and let the painting fall. As she walked away, she trod on it and the painted paper stuck to her shoe. She only got as far as the door when Celina tripped over to her.

"My dear, my dear, your artwork." She tapped Nettie's leg and retrieved the painting. Celina carried the painting to the shelf singing to it as she did.

"Dear Picasso, are you turning in your grave?" I murmured.

"Finish up, finish up," Celina crooned. Henry stopped painting his horse. It was a lovely strawberry colour. I could see Arthur Proctor putting little finishing touches to his nude woman. He had put high heel shoes on her and added a bit to her chest. I pretended to add little touches to my painting as though I knew what I was doing. Celina gathered up our finished work.

"Tomorrow, tomorrow," she warbled. I waited and put my painting right at the top of the pile. I intend to steal it and work on it when no one is looking.

Nov. 29th

Early this morning before the activity people came to work I snuck in and got my painting. I had to try and improve it. I'd love to have it hanging somewhere, even in the quiet room. I went to find Joe, the Janitor. He looked at it and, without a word, gave me some cleaning fluid and an old rag. I tried to clean off some of the colours so that I could start again, but the cleaning fluid only made the paint run together. I tried turning the sheet over but the colours had run through to the back. I gave Joe his cleaning fluid back. He tried to cheer me up.

"You know, Picasso had to start somewhere," he told me. "Just tell the judge that." Joe looked at the paper with its streaks of integrated colours. He held it up to the light and we could clearly see through the holes where I had rubbed too hard with the cleaning fluid. "Let them think you did that on purpose," he suggested, "and tell them this was your 'washed out' period." Joe is quite a philosopher; you really need input from friends at a time like this.

I decided that Joe was so right that I glued sequins from my sewing box all around the edges of the 'washed out' holes. Then I took it back to the activity room.

Nov. 30th

When we went to art class today, all our paintings were hanging on the activity room wall. I could see that everyone was as excited as I was. We walked around looking at each other's paintings. The Dolly Sisters' pictures were hanging next to each other, probably because they had done a picture of half a tree each. When you looked at them side by side, you saw a finished tree. But it looked as though it had been struck by lightning; it was completely bare.

"It's November, we couldn't paint any leaves," one explained.

"No, we couldn't paint any leaves," said the other.

Henry's horse looked magnificent. Even Arthur's nude lady looked better from a distance. Quite a few people seemed to have painted jars of flowers. I noticed a picture of a sunset that looked a lot like a fried egg. Some man I only know by sight had painted something that looked like a rat holding an eagle up by its legs. The man was a bit annoyed.

"You've got it upside down," he shouted. They put it right; I thought it looked more interesting the other way.

Henry hugged me when he saw my picture. "Clover," he said, "you're way ahead of your time."

A young man in the loudest shirt I have ever seen came through the door.

"Sebastian, Sebastian." Celina ran over and kissed him. "Our judge, our judge." Celina motioned us to sit down. Without a word, Sebastian looked at the paintings. He walked, rather like a ballet dancer, over to the wall. He stopped and made comments at each one.

"Good, good," he said, as he tapped Henry's horse. "Flesh and blood," he said to Arthur's nude. At the Dolly Sister's tree painting he turned and looked at Celina. "Ah hah, schizophrenic... very interesting." He looked long and hard at Nellie's artwork. "Hmmm," and in a questioning voice he said, "Under the influence of..." as he passed on.

I hardly dare look as he stopped at my painting. He moved his finger over the sequins, "I don't care for these," he said, "but this, this and this..." He moved his hand all around the washed out holes. He turned to us. "Who did this?" he asked. I stepped nervously forward. "How did you get this movement of colour?" He asked. "This great capricious kaleidoscopic? The pigment and colouration? How did you do this?" I tried to think of the name of the cleaning fluid Joe had given me.

"Um...I can't tell you..."

"Fine, fine, we all have our little secrets." He shook his finger at me, then he handed Celina my picture, and two others. He blew her a kiss and was gone.

Joe, the Janitor, was so pleased to see my picture in the quiet room this evening. It was hanging in the middle of the wall. On one side was a picture of the back alley. It was pretty dark and dismal I thought. On the other side of my painting was a picture of a sunflower.

"Yours makes the other two look mundane," he said.

He's really with it, is Joe.

December

Dec. 1st

Today, me and Henry were poking around in Nellie's Twice Upon a Time store. Nellie has never forgiven me for the April Fool joke I played on her. Some people just have no sense of humour! Nellie scowled at me and, as usual smiled sweetly at Henry. I reached over and pointed to a pair of earrings, a pink elephant dangling from each one.

"They're already spoken for," she snapped.

"Well, all I can say is some people have very poor taste," I told her. She got uppity.

"All this stuff is my own private collection, I'll have you know." She acted like she was the Queen showing off the crown jewels. I was going to tell her that I wouldn't be seen dead in any of it, when I became aware of something glinting at the edge of the table. It was a huge diamond ring. It had eight little stones surrounding a great big one; the large stone was as big as a green pea.

"Oh, Henry, look!" He picked it up.

"Would you like it, Clover?" he asked. Nellie leaned forward, glaring at me.

"It's not cheap. And anyway I don't think it will suit you," she scoffed.

"Look," said Henry, "I don't care what it costs. If Clover wants it she can have it. How much?" Nellie's lips tightened.

"Nine dollars," she muttered. I saw red.

"Nine dollars!" I snatched the ring out of Henry's hand. Somehow it slipped through my fingers, bounced on the floor then came to rest. Nellie peered over the edge of the counter. The huge middle stone had fallen out.

"You broke it, Clover!" she shrieked, "Look at the sign! If you break it you've bought it!"

"Okay, okay," said Henry. He got out a ten-dollar bill.

"Just a minute," I said. "It's going to cost us a couple of dollars to get some crazy glue to fix it. We'll give you seven dollars."

"Seven fifty," she shot back. Henry gave her the money without argument.

He's a real soft touch.

Dec. 6th

I showed my ring to Joe, the Janitor. He has solved so many of my problems.

"I've got some glue," he said. "It's not crazy glue but it's just stubborn enough to keep that stone on." Then he cleaned it for me with some special soap.

When Joe had finished, it looked so good I said to Henry. "Let's have it appraised. You know, it could be worth at least fifty dollars I bet."

"I doubt that," said Henry. "But it does look good on you, Clover, you give it class."

Henry has more taste than anyone I know.

Dec. 8th

I don't know whether the petition had anything to do with it, but Sidney our cook came in today. He said hi to us over the intercom while we were having lunch. He told us he would be back cooking for us soon. He's on parole from his bigamy conviction. His lady parole officer even came with him. He seemed really proud to show her his kitchen. We asked him to stay for lunch, but he took one look at Lorylee's open-faced tuna and spinach sandwiches and declined.

"Couldn't you get Lorylee a job cooking in the prison system?" I asked Sidney,

"No," he said. "Not unless you want to see a prison riot."

Dec. 11th

Me and Henry walked down to Birks jewellery store on Granville Street today to have my ring appraised. I looked around for someone to help us. I saw a gentleman with nice white hair.

"We'll ask him, Henry," I suggested. "He looks as though he would know all about antiques."

"Right," said Henry, "cause he is one."

"We would like an appraisal of my diamond ring, if you don't mind," I told the man. He stopped polishing the glass counter.

"Come and sit down." He waved at three chairs near a small table by the window. He sat down and we sat across from him. He put a funny glass thing to one eye, then pointed at a lovely purple cushion between us. I grinned at Henry and placed my ring in the centre of the cushion. With a flourish he lifted the ring. He held the ring about two inches from his eye and gazed at it through the glass thing. Suddenly the little glass thing fell out of his eye. He stared at both of us for a moment.

"Good God! You have to be..." His face went the colour of undercooked roast beef, then he fell backwards; chair and all. The terrible thing was that my ring went flying up in the air and out of sight. Half a dozen members of the staff came running over. They had heard the thud as he hit the floor.

"Mr. Van Gurder! Mr. Van Gurder!" A young woman came from behind the nearest counter, knelt by his side and gently tapped his face.

"I'll get an ambulance," someone shouted.

"Yes! Yes!" the young woman answered. "It has to be another heart attack." In seconds a young man was there. He looked into the senseless face of Mr. Van Gurder, then spoke in a whisper to the young woman.

"Get my father." She ran to the back of the store. The young man was now kneeling beside Mr. Van Gurder.

"Don't move," he whispered. "They've gone for Mr. Clapperhorn." Me and Henry got up from our chairs.

"Should we get out of here, Clover?" Henry asked.

"Not without my ring," I told him. Soon a very important looking man walked over. The woman with him wore a gold identity pin, which said Miss Miller. Someone put a rolled up coat under Mr. Van Gurder's head. The impressive-looking man came over to us.

"Could I have a word with you? I'm the manager, Mr. Clapperhorn." He said it as though he was announcing the six o'clock news. An ambulance arrived and we waited while Mr. Van Gurder was put gently on a stretcher. He began to moan and Henry grabbed my arm as I moved toward the stretcher to ask about my ring. When the ambulance men had taken the stretcher through the door, Mr. Clapperhorn turned back to me and Henry.

"I believe Mr. Van Gurder was helping you with some transaction when…this unfortunate incident occurred? Did he appear… distressed or anything to you?"

"Well, all I can say," I said, "is that he must have been over-whelmed by my ring." Miss Miller and the young man and woman were listening. They closed in on us.

"Precisely what ring are we talking about?" asked the manager.

"Well," I said, "he just looked at this ring we showed him and he said 'Good God,' didn't he Henry?" Henry nodded.

"Then he sort of gasped," Henry said.

I tried to think back. "Oh, and then he said...'you have got to be...' and I think he was just going to say 'millionaires,' don't you, Henry?"

"You never know, you never know," said Henry. I looked at the serious faces of the staff. The young man looked startled. Like a child who'd been told there's no Santa Claus.

Then, I went on. "He just keeled over."

"I will be happy to finalize the transaction," said Mr. Clapper horn. He motioned us to the little table again.

"Well, that's the problem," said Henry, "We don't know where the ring is."

"You see, Mr. Van Gurder dropped it," I told him. "He was so amazed when he saw it...it had the same effect on us when we bought it, didn't it, Henry?"

"Yes," said Henry, "it was a sparkler alright." The four assistants were now looking on the floor around the small table.

"Miss Miller," announced Mr. Clapperhorn, "lock the doors till we find the ring." He seemed quite nervous. Miss Miller went over to a young couple standing by the counter and whispered something. They followed her to the door. Mr. Clapperhorn turned to the staff who were still searching the area.

"It has to be somewhere," he snapped. "Look around, look around." He came up close to me and Henry and in a soft voice he said, "Did Mr. Van Gurder mention money? Did he say what his appraisal of the ring was, perhaps?"

"No, he didn't get round to that," I answered.

"Do you mind...uh...telling me what the cost of the ring was?" Mr. Clapperhorn bent his head as though he was a priest in a confessional box. Henry answered.

"Well, it was more than we were prepared to give, but you know...Clover liked it and that was it." I was trying to add up seven fifty and the price of the glue.

"A lot more than we bargained for," I added. Mr. Clapperhorn looked up at the ceiling for a long time, he seemed to be praying. I reminded Henry that the video *Casablanca*, was on our big TV screen at two o'clock and they'd have to look for the ring without us.

"Feel free to go," said the manager in a really icy tone. "I assure you we will find the ring." He looked angrily at the assistants. The young man was looking under the purple cushion with quivering hands. Miss Miller was shaking the curtains. The young woman had moved the table and chairs out of the way. Mr. Clapperhorn walked with us to the door.

"About the price again," he said softly, "Would it have been perhaps...uh...in the three, four figure range would you say?" he looked at us as though his life depended on the answer. I looked at Henry for help.

"Maybe more like seven something," I told him. He grabbed the handle of the door as though to steady himself. "Well, goodbye," I said. "When you find the ring, phone Honeystone Mansion, they're in the phone book. Tell them you've found Clover Rayton's diamond ring. I'll let them know you'll be phoning."

Yes, I thought to myself, I'd like to see all their faces when that's announced over the intercom at Honeystone.

Henry and me enjoyed *Casablanca*. We both really identify with Ingrid Bergman and Humphrey Bogart. Sometimes Henry will say with a funny Humphrey Bogart lisp, "Clover, we'll always have Honeystone." But instead of crying like Ingrid Bergman, I laugh.

Dec. 12th

I like being a member of The Problem Solving Committee; however, I have neglected to solve anything lately. One of my New Year resolutions will be to solve everyone's problems. I even intend to solve young Dr. Whitaker's problem. He gives us bimonthly lectures on 'sexual activity in the elderly.' He constantly keeps breaking into a coughing spell, particularly when Arthur Proctor asks questions; Arthur never gets an answer. Only last month Arthur asked two simple questions. One was about Osteoporosis, for heaven sake!

"Is it alright," Arthur asked, "to jump somebody's bones when they're eighty-two? My second question is, at what point are our bones going to crack?"

I thought Dr. Whitaker was going to have an apoplectic fit. He coughed so much he had to leave the room. Either he needs cough drops, or a chat about the birds and bees. I would tell him that he's wasting his time, but he has a nice voice and the chairs are comfy for sleeping. In order to help him I'll also use one of my many life-improving quotes. This one is from *The King and I.* "When you become a teacher, by your pupils you'll be taught."

Dec. 13th

I thought maybe I should practice some problem solving today. It wasn't exactly a success. I decided for Christmas that everyone should have nice clean, shiny teeth. I found a big plastic bowl and filled it with warm water and bleach. I didn't get too much on the carpet. I swished my own partial denture first and put them right back in. I have to look my best because I'm head of the committee; well, I'm the only one doing it. I got Arthur Proctor's teeth and Henry's partial plate. The Dolly Sisters had five small dentures between them, not one of the dentures had more than two teeth on them. The rest of their 'real teeth' looked like tiny crooked gravestones scattered around their mouths. I managed to pry the teeth out of the mouth of Monster. Nettie Spooner had to look for hers; she was having one of those 'out of body' days. We finally found them lodged inside her brassiere. By the time I got around to everyone on the fourth floor, the bottom of the bowl was nicely full of teeth.

I used the big bathroom by the nursing station; it was peaceful and quiet. I swished the teeth around with my chopstick, it's a useful thing. I often use it for knocking things off shelves that are too high and for propping open my window. I watched the teeth becoming whiter and then I realized something was wrong. All the teeth looked similar. I knew I might not be solving a problem; in fact I might have a problem. I rinsed off the teeth and then I took the easy teeth back first. The Dolly Sisters only took twenty minutes to sort their teeth out. Henry had a gold tooth at the front of his denture. I had polished it till it shone like a star. As for the rest, I invited them to my room. Putting the bowl of dentures on my little table, I told them there was a prize for the one who found their teeth first.

"Spill the beans, Clover," said Arthur Proctor. Some of his words were shushy without his teeth. "You've done something real stupid, haven't you?"

"Arthur," I replied, "I want to bring a little fun and joy into your life, is that so bad?"

"Well, the prize had better be good, that's all," he said as he pushed through to the front, knocking Nettie Spooner over, which is never difficult to do. Arthur then started a fight with Mr. Marlow. He wanted to keep Mr. Marlow's teeth because, as Arthur said, "they make me look like Tom Cruise." They soon stopped wrestling when I sprayed them both with my bug-off can. Finally everyone was satisfied and I gave all of them a jelly bean from my Christmas candy jar. I told them they were all winners.

The whole room was pretty messy when they'd finished. I noticed the bleach stains on the rug. Well, I thought, I might as well have one last fight with Snerd the cost clerk before the end of the year. Then I noticed at the bottom of the bowl, one more denture. I knew it had to belong to Monster. I went to see him, but he was fast asleep. I propped his mouth open by putting a wad of paper tissue at one side. He didn't wake. I then managed with some effort to get his denture into his mouth sideways. This, I said to myself, is a problem someone else will have to solve. Quickly I went to Judy at the nurse's desk. It happens that everybody knows that Monster has never spoken a word since he arrived. Judy was busy writing in the Doctor's book.

"I think I heard Monster saying 'The Lord's Prayer' as I went by his room," I told her. Judy leapt to her feet and shrieked.

"At last! And on my shift!" She flew to his room. I watched her open his door. A second later I heard another shriek. This one reminded me of the sound the woman made when she first saw the *Phantom of the Opera* without his mask.

Dec. 14th

Miss Miller from Birks called today. They want to see me and Henry. I hope they've found my ring; I'd like to wear it for Christmas. I've been wondering how Mr. Van Gurder is, and whether I should pop in to St. Paul's Hospital and see him.

Dec. 15th

Me and Henry went down to Birks today. All of the staff were really polite. Miss Miller and a very young man who was a lot prettier than Miss Miller took us into a room at the back. Miss Miller's face was quite pink when she said, "We are so sorry. We just haven't located the ring." She looked at both our faces as though expecting to be attacked. The young man ran his fingers through his blond curls and moved slightly closer to her side. Without taking her eyes off us, Miss Miller bent and lifted a tray of rings onto the desk in front of us. She reminded me of a puppet on a string. Her smile kept appearing then disappearing. They both looked down reverently at the ring tray, as though they were showing us a favourite relative's body in a morgue. The young man wore one glistening earring. I wondered where the other one was. Did they lose that too?

Miss Miller asked timidly, "Would you mind looking at this tray of rings?" Me and Henry stepped forward.

"Well, we're looking," said Henry, "but I don't see the point."

"We'd just like an idea of what..." she looked at the young man who finished her sentence.

"...your ring looked like." I had no hesitation in making a decision and answering them.

"There, that one there! Exactly like that...right, Henry?" I was pointing to the biggest ring in the tray.

"I'm sure you're right, Clover."

"But," I said, "I hope you're not palming us off with that, because I want my own ring." I gave Henry a smile. "It has very sentimental value for me."

"Of course, of course," Miss Miller whispered. She sadly put the tray away. The young man's eyes looked misty. I felt like hugging him. Miss Miller walked us to the door.

"We're having special people in with detectors," she told us confidentially, as though the CIA had something to do with the search.

"Yes, good, just find it," I said. "We've been more than patient, you know. By the way, how's Mr. Van Gurder?" She seemed glad to change the subject.

"I wish I could say he's well, but he seems to be in a coma."

"I'll pop in," I said. "He probably just needs his mind jogging a bit." Miss Miller shook her head furiously and opened her mouth to speak. I hadn't time to chat. We had to go shop for Christmas decorations.

Dec. 16th

We all have been looking forward to the Christmas Lights ride. Honeystone Mansion puts on this bus ride every year. I got our gang together on the fourth floor and gave everyone a Christmas carol songbook. On our way to the front door we sang "Rudolf the Red Nosed Reindeer," the first carol in the book. Monster didn't sing. He used his song sheet to blow his nose.

Not many people were waiting at the front door, which surprised me, although I knew we were a bit early. Our sightseeing bus, which only holds ten people, wasn't in sight. The only vehicle standing there was a large tour bus. Well, maybe we're going in style for a change, I thought.

The Dolly Sisters climbed on board first, carrying their little toy binoculars round their necks. I followed them with Henry. I had to give the twins a little push; they had stopped to smile and chat to the bus driver who was busy adjusting his seat. I put my scarf beside Henry on the front seat, "I'll just go and make sure everyone's getting on okay," I told him.

A care aide brought Maisey along and helped her up the steps, then put her folding walker beside her. Maisey promised not to fall. The driver still didn't take notice as I got Monster comfortably settled behind me and Henry. Nettie Spooner arrived, having one of her usual 'out of body' experiences. I noticed the driver had now finished adjusting his seat and he was taking an interest in what was going on. He gazed with awe at Nettie as she sailed by him on her way to the back seat, the one where she would eventually have to lie down. Little did the driver know her long cape hid the bag of special cookies essential to her existence. She'd obviously eaten some of them already. She settled herself and asked, "When do we arrive in Las Vegas?"

The driver quickly picked up his schedule and scanned it. Arthur Proctor was now on board and he sat across from the twins. Arthur borrowed their binoculars alternately, whenever a young girl went by. I looked around at the empty seats left on the bus. It seemed a pity to waste them. I noticed my old friend Willy the bag man sitting on the street bench near the front door.

"Hey," I shouted, "do you want to come for a drive?" Willy picked up two green plastic bags he always carries. He struggled on board. When the driver told him that luggage had to go under the bus, Willy replied, "These bags never leave my side."

The driver didn't get a chance to argue, because I had hailed two old ladies that were just passing by. They happily tottered on the bus passed him. The driver kept referring to his clipboard. When I finally sat down beside Henry, I said to the driver,

"Well, we're ready when you are." The driver turned to me with a puzzled expression. I guess he thought I was the leader; a common mistake.

"Is this the Honeystone Mansion Christmas group?" he asked as he looked again at his clipboard.

"Of course we're the Honeystone Christmas group."

"But it's only ten after six," he replied.

"So?" I asked.

"Well we're not supposed to leave till six thirty."

"Look," I pointed out, "we're all here, that's all that matters. Let's go!"

We continued with our song sheet as the driver started up the engine. As we left the curb I looked back. Judy, the fourth floor nurse, had just come flying out of the front door. I noticed she was quite dressed up. I also recognized the care aides and staff who followed her. Rhodena was amongst them. They were all dressed up in fancy clothes. They waved excitedly at the bus as it pulled away; some were jumping up and down and shouting. That's nice of them to see us off, I thought as I waved back.

We had nearly finished everything on our song sheet when the bus stopped.

"I wonder why we're stopping at the Parkside Inn?" I said to Henry. He was on the fourth verse of "Good King Wenceslas." He stopped singing when a young uniformed man opened the door and climbed in.

"Good evening, I'm Bill. Are you the Honeystone Mansion group?"

"We certainly are," I answered. He looked at us and frowned. He glanced at the driver, the driver shrugged.

"And you're here for the Christmas banquet?" he went on.

"We're here for everything we can get," shouted Arthur Proctor. Everyone got up at the sound of the word banquet. Young uniformed Bill backed up to the door. He looked a bit scared as we all moved toward him. As the Dolly Sisters passed him, one or the other of them whacked him on the shoulder with her binoculars, he ducked and the second twin accidentally hit him on the head with her binoculars. We were nearly all off the bus when Bill, rubbing his head, called to another man in uniform at the front door of the Parkside.

"Charlie, this lot's for the Queen Charlotte Room."

"This lot?"

"Yes." Unfortunately Bill was now standing on the bottom step of the bus. He hadn't seen Monster trying to get off the bus behind him. I waved to warn Bill. He turned and gave a little shriek as Monster waved back at me. Bill got another swipe over the head from Monster, then staggered and fell off the bottom step.

Charlie had thick white hair. He was much older than Bill. He looked as though he had served in the Crimean War; he even had medals on his chest. Charlie held the big front doors open and he hardly glanced at us as we filed through. The last of us to come through the door was Willy with his plastic bags. Charlie did notice the bags. He looked at Willy as though he'd caught him going AWOL. Charlie grabbed Willy's two plastic bags. Young Bill had now followed us in.

"Here, Bill, take these to the cloak room." Bill held the bags away from his body as though they contained something live. Willy watched sadly as his whole life's possessions were carried off. Charlie then commanded us like a sergeant major.

"Walk this way." Arthur Proctor did an exaggerated imitation of the way Charlie walked. He swung his arms vigorously and marched behind him. We all laughed and followed. The Dolly Sisters looked at the oil paintings on the walls using their binoculars. There was a scramble when we had to rescue a large piece of artwork from Monster. It was made of stone and in the shape of a horn full of real fruit.

Charlie and Bill then opened the double doors of the Queen Charlotte Room. It was gorgeous. A long table had been decorated and set for about twenty people. Every now and then along the table was a bottle of wine. We admired everything for a few seconds and then we each found a seat we liked and sat down. Henry's artificial leg creaked and we laughed.

"This is the best Christmas Lights tour I've ever been on," I whispered to Henry. Food started to appear as half a dozen waitresses came in. I realized I was quite hungry. Someone poured wine for us. Henry was at the head of the table so they served him first, asking him if the wine was alright.

"We'll let you know after a few glasses," he said. The two old ladies I had picked up on the street pulled the Christmas crackers that were set in front them. Everyone then did the same, there was a lot of banging and laughing, and we all wound up with paper hats from inside the crackers. Then Arthur Proctor stood up to make a speech.

"Christmas brings out the best in people," he began. We applauded. "Look how nice we all are," he swept his glass of wine around the table spilling a bit down Nettie Spooner's chiffon dress. She hardly noticed. Nettie was zonked. "So," Arthur went on, "let's thank the good Lord for this lovely..." he swept his arm around once more and the remaining wine got Nettie again.

"Whoops!" was all she said as she slid to the floor.

"Yes," Arthur was in full swing, he pointed with his empty glass at the table, "this is human nature at its finest." As he said this, a man we had never seen before came bustling into the room. He was wearing a tuxedo and had a thin moustache; he reminded me of a tango teacher I once knew.

"There's been a terrible mistake. I must ask you to–"

"Just ask us anything you like." Arthur Proctor's voice was getting slurry.

"Leave!" the strange man shouted. "There's been a mistake. You have to leave."

"This is no way to treat customers, you know," I said. "I doubt if any of us will ever come here again."

"That is a risk I am willing to take," he barked.

Everyone stood quietly but no one was moving away from the table. Arthur Proctor picked up two wine bottles and put them into his deep jacket pockets. The Dolly Sisters filled their purses with the decorations from the table. The tuxedo man waved at the waitresses, who started huffily clearing the table. Bill and Charlie came back on the scene.

"Bunch of impostors." I heard one of them mutter. Then Willy, the old man, spoke.

"I want my matching luggage."

"What matching luggage?" Charlie shouted back.

"My two green plastic bags," Willy shouted back. Bill came in with the bags and handed them over. Willy began throwing everything that was left on the table into the bags. It took both Bill and Charlie to wrestle Willy and the bags through the door. When Nettie Spooner appeared from under the table she saw the food being taken away.

"What a lovely party it was," she said as Arthur Proctor helped her to the door.

Monster must have thought something sad was going on because he started to cry. He picked up the edge of the white linen tablecloth to wipe his eyes and blow his nose. Bill and Charlie were now standing to attention and holding open the big double doors. We all moved toward them with as much pride as we could muster. As we went through the door I could hear behind us the sound of crashing and smashing. I looked back. Monster was still holding on to the tablecloth and dragging it with him, as water jugs, glasses, and cutlery fell to the floor behind him. He walked through the foyer looking like a very tall, ugly bride trailing a long, stained, bridal train. I went back to him, loosened Monster's fingers from the tablecloth. We were now heading outside. The tuxedo man was standing by the door. As I passed, I noticed some beautiful chocolates on lovely silver trays on the sideboard; I poured one of the trays into my handbag as I went by. Finally we heard the big door slam behind us.

Our bus driver was hopping up and down outside his bus.

"Come on, come on, come on," he snapped. "I've got to get back for the real group."

"Hey," I said, "this is as real as it gets. Here–have a chocolate!"

When we got back to Honeystone the two old ladies thanked us and asked when the next bus trip would be. Willy came in and joined us. He shared some of the food that he picked up at the Parkside. Clive, our evening care aide, lit us a fire in the lounge and said, "Well, you lot shouldn't be surprised if the staff aren't speaking to you tomorrow. Fancy hijacking their bus and gatecrashing their party!"

We all laughed and drank the rest of the wine and sang a few more carols. Monster looked like a huge happy child. Clive took him off to bed. Then he came back with a wheelchair to take Nettie off to her room.

I leaned over to Henry and said, "You'd think the administration could manage to organize a simple Christmas outing without totally messing up wouldn't you?" Henry just shrugged his shoulder and smiled. The rest of us stayed by the fire and the last thing I remembered was the night supervisor waking us all up and telling us to go to bed.

Dec. 17th

The ambulance came today to take Mollie Harris to St. Paul's Hospital. She had to have her blood checked because she keeps having dizzy spells. I could have told them about the Five Star Whiskey she has in the bottom drawer of her dresser, but we all like an outing once in a while, so I told them she needed me to come with her because I was her best friend. I don't really like the woman, but I wanted to go see Mr. Van Gurder.

When we got to St. Paul's I went straight to the information desk. I gave the young woman a run down on the events leading up to Mr. Van Gurder's arrival by ambulance. When she'd finished yawning, she told me where to find him. A smart looking older woman wearing a lovely mauve outfit was hovering over Mr. Van Gurder. He lay quite still. The woman patted his face with a lacy pocket hanky. A young man in a really nice navy suit, who I gathered was Mr. Van Gurder's son, stood beside her. I called over from the doorway.

"Mr. Van Gurder? Mr. Van Gurder? I just wondered about my ring." He immediately opened his eyes. He stared for a moment at the ceiling as though he'd heard the voice of an angel. Then his expression changed to a look of terror. He moved his head in my direction.

"No, no," he shook his head. The mauve lady waved her hanky in the air.

"Ring? Ring? What does she mean, Wolfgang? Did you give this woman a ring?"

"No, no," I told her, "I gave him a ring." The mauve lady made a sound as though someone had stuck a pin in her.

"No, go away." Mr. Van Gurder had rolled over to face me. He was leaning on one elbow. I never give up easily.

"I will not be put off like this, Mr. Van Gurder," I said.

"You shameless woman," the mauve lady shouted at me.

"Does it matter what she is, Mother?" the young man said, "I mean, look, Dad was in a coma, she brought him back to life."

"And I might put him to death," the woman said, flicking her hanky. A nurse came up behind me and gently pushed me aside to get through the doorway. The young man was shaking with excitement.

"It's okay, it's okay," he kept saying. Mr. Van Gurder was warding off blows from the small lace hanky.

"Excuse me," said the nurse as she put her hand on Mr. Van Gurder's wrist. "Good, he's coming out of it," she said. Mr. Van Gurder gave a weak smile. I waved and called over to him.

"I want my ring back for Christmas, so snap out of it." Mr. Van Gurder threw back the sheets and struggled to his feet. The nurse and the young man tried to restrain him. Frankly speaking, his hospital gown was a little shorter than I would have preferred. He was now standing and breathing heavily. He looked like a Brahma bull about to charge.

The mauve lady picked up the chart attached to a metal hook at the base of bed. She headed toward me. Her son was helping the nurse to wrestle his dad back on to the bed. I quickly waved goodbye, but I shouted back to Mr. Van Gurder,

"I'll be happy to talk about this later." I headed down the hall. I could hear voices all the way to the elevator. "How could you, Wolfgang?" and the young man saying over and over,

"This is good, Mother, this is good."

I went to find Molly. She was in her wheelchair at the front door. "Let's get back to Honeystone, Clover," she said. "I'm dying for a drink."

"I think I'll have one with you," I told her. "I reckon I deserve one. I've just performed a miracle upstairs on a man who was at death's door."

Dec. 18th

It looks like we're stuck with our horrible cook Lorylee for a while longer. We've had a postcard from Sidney, our former great cook, and he's in Kelowna. We might have to wait a bit longer to get him back. I passed the postcard around on the fourth floor. The card was from the Best Western Hotel. Rhodena tells me the administration office received a letter saying that Sidney had run off with his parole officer.

Dec. 19th

I phoned St. Paul's Hospital today to ask about Mr. Van Gurder; they told me he had gone home.

"Did he ever talk numbers in his sleep?" I asked. "You know, like money and stuff?"

"We would never divulge things of that nature," the snooty voice said.

"Do you have his home number?" I asked.

She said, "No we can't divulge that either."

This might become a police matter. Christmas is coming soon. I really want my ring.

Dec. 20th

I cheered up today because my grandson Sandy took me to see the Christmas windows at the Bay; they were lovely as usual. He drove me to all the big hotels and we saw the Christmas trees in all the foyers. I explained to Sandy how my friends and I missed seeing the Christmas lights.

"Imagine, getting us onto the wrong bus like that," I told him. Sandy promised to take Henry and me to see the lights next week. Sandy also took me to the Cathedral on Pender Street. The Christmas nativity scene was so lovely I wanted everyone at Honeystone Mansion to see it. Sandy said that when he comes tomorrow to help decorate my room we'll plan a trip for the gang to go to the Cathedral.

Dec. 21st

They found my ring at Birks. The people who look after their plants found it in the soil of a rubber plant. Birks sent it in an envelope with their name on it. I hope everyone heard when Diane announced it on the intercom.

"Jewellery from Birks for Clover Rayton," she said. I went to the desk to thank her. I reached over and turned the intercom back on, then I spoke nice and clearly.

"Thanks, Diane," I said, "it's a diamond ring they've been assessing for me; it took a while because it's a very special ring." Diane reached over and turned off the intercom.

"Why don't you take out an ad in the paper so the whole world will know?"

"That's not a bad idea," I told her. When I got to my room I found there was a note inside from Mr. Clapperhorn. They're threatening to take legal action, something about being a public nuisance. I wrote back and told them I'd never buy another thing from their store.

Dec. 22nd

Sandy and I did a wonderful job decorating my room. He brought about fifty coloured balloons. He was a bit purple by the time he'd blown them up, but he had enough energy to stand on a chair and after rubbing them on his sweater, "to give them friction," he stuck them on the ceiling. We put sprigs of holly from his garden all over my dresser and TV.

Dec. 23rd

The friction holding the balloons up is wearing off. This morning they started coming loose from the ceiling. Every few minutes a balloon would drift down. Unfortunately they always seemed to land on a sprig of holly. I was ready each time for the bang, but Maisey wasn't. From behind the partition she kept giving little shrieks. I tried to be helpful and warn her as they floated down. "Okay, get ready...now." She still screamed. After about twenty balloons, the nurse had to give her a tranquilizer.

Dec. 24th

It was one of the most exciting Christmases I've had since I was a child. My grandson Sandy borrowed the car. He made two trips to the Cathedral on Pender Street. He took the Dolly Sisters and Arthur Proctor on one trip. Then he took me and Henry and Monster on the second trip. After a quick look at the nativity scene, Sandy sat down on the front pew to eat one of the apples his mother had sent for me.

The figures of Mary and Joseph and the animals were almost life-size. The Dolly Sisters walked in and out of the scene stroking the sheep and the ox. They had a little conversation with the donkey about the trip to Bethlehem. They told the donkey how they'd been to Jerusalem but were too late to see Jesus. Arthur Proctor spent his time scrutinizing the nearly nude cherubs that hovered above the stable. Henry speculated on what kind of wood had been used for the figures. Monster, all seven foot of him, lumbered around smiling but without speaking as always. He lifted one of the three wise men and gazed into his face as though looking at some large family photo. Then he saw the tiny child in the manger. He gave Joseph a shove, picked Mary up and leaned her against an ox. He opened his arms and staggered forward.

"Baby, baby," he said.

"Did you hear that?" I asked in a loud whisper. "It's a miracle. That's the first time he's ever spoken." We were so flabbergasted we didn't try to stop him when he lifted the baby out of the wooden manger.

"Jesus," whispered Henry beside me.

"Christ," said Arthur Proctor.

"Will you two stop taking the Lord's name in vain?" I said. "And you," I looked up at Monster, "for God's sakes put that baby back." He didn't seem to hear me. He swayed back and forth. The Dolly Sisters didn't help either; they started singing 'Rock a Bye Baby.' I heard the sound of people coming through the front door of the cathedral.

"Quick," I said, "let's go. We'll figure out what to do later." Sandy jumped up from the front pew and pointed to the side door that led out onto the alley. He held it open for us. As Monster passed him with the baby, Sandy gave him a gentle dig.

"So...who's the lucky lady?"

"Baby, baby..." Monster was drooling. We hadn't realized that when he picked up the baby, he had also picked up an armful of hay. We were leaving a trail right through the side door and onto the street.

"Sandy," I asked, "do you think you can get everyone back to Honeystone? I'll go to the drugstore over there and buy a doll or something for the manger."

"No sweat," said Sandy. He told them all to stay just where they were and he would bring the car around.

I headed across the road to The Mighty Midget Drugstore and went straight to the toy counter where a young girl was straightening the boxes on the shelves. It didn't seem as though there were many toys left.

"So," I said casually, trying to hide the fact that I was desperate, "what's new in dolls this year?"

"Well," the girl said, "we've just got a few old styles of Barbie left." She came down from her ladder. "We've got this," she placed a glossy package on the table. Proudly, she said, "It's Barbie goes Hawaiian." Then she handed across another package. "And this... Barbie plays tennis." I looked at the doll with its thin torso and big chest.

"Um, no. I need a boy doll," I said. The girl seemed a little taken aback.

"Well, we do have this," she produced another package. "This is Barbie and Ken at Club Med."

"Oh... I think he might do," I said. The girl looked a bit strangely at me.

"I suppose he does look cute in that outfit," she answered.

"Well, that doesn't matter," I told her, "I'll be taking his clothes off. I don't suppose you've got a bigger boy than Ken?" She took a step back, bumping her head on the ladder.

"Are you sure you're in the right kind of shop, Madam?" she stammered. I could see that time was getting on. I wondered what was happening back at the Cathedral.

"Yes. Definitely," I said. "I want him!" I broke the plastic before the girl could stop me and pulled Ken from the package.

"You can't leave Barbie alone like that...they're a pair," she wailed.

"I'll pay for both," I told her as I pulled Ken's clothes off. She ran to a door marked Staff Only. I peeled off the price sticker and stuck it on Ken's stomach. Then I went over to the checkout girl. She wasn't as sensitive as the first clerk. She never questioned why Ken was wearing nothing but shoes and socks. I dropped the money on the counter, grabbed the doll and hurried back to the Cathedral.

A well-dressed couple with a small child passed me as I hurried down the aisle. They seemed rather upset. I stopped to let them pass. The little girl was looking up at her parents and saying,

"Jesus isn't there because Jesus wasn't borned yet, 'cause it's not Christmas yet." Her father looked down at her impatiently.

"Born. The word is born!" He pulled the little girl along. The mother glanced back at the nativity scene. "I just hope that Polly has not been permanently damaged by the sight of that empty manger."

I waited till the front door to the Cathedral closed behind them. Then I quickly ripped off Ken's shoes and socks and buried him in what was left of the hay. I muttered a quick prayer asking for forgiveness and saying I would bring back the Christ Child as soon as I could.

Feeling quite weary after all the excitement I headed home. As I strolled along I recalled all that had happened and couldn't help but reflect on the year that had just passed. I remembered how angry I was last Christmas when my children announced they were sending me to Honeystone Mansion.

But now, even though the food needs improvement and the administration seems to always need my help, I realize I'm happy. And I'm very pleased to know that Honeystone is my new home, and the people there, especially my favourite friends, are my new family.

Thanks

To the Scribblers Writing group for their encouragement to publish *Everything's Coming Up Clover* and for their undying love and affection for Dora. Special thanks to Rosselind Sexton, without her support and love this project would never have taken flight! Thanks to the Preston, Rayton, and Blackburn families for their committed support and love. Also, to the countless friends always ready and willing to help. Thanks to the publishing houses that provided praise and encouragement to bring this book to the readers of the world, even though they didn't want to do it. Thanks to Haro Park Centre for providing the landscape for Clover's adventures. And last, but not least, thanks to Dora, for making everyone's life shine brighter....we miss you.

Acknowledgements

Rosselind Sexton for contributing endless hours of editing and review. Glenys Preston Blackburn for her dedication to see the publication process through. Ann Westlake, Editor-in-Chief at Writer's Cramp Editing Consultants. Stephen Rayton for the digital sound track.

About the Author

DORA PRESTON 1926 ~ 2011 was born in Leeds, Yorkshire, England. After marrying in the 1950's, Dora and her husband John made their way to Canada, settling in southern Ontario where they raised two children. Dora worked a variety of jobs, but eventually she found her calling, settling in as a care aide. In addition to her career, and raising a family, Dora's life as a writer remained central. Her poetry and short stories have appeared in magazines, literary journals and newspapers, winning her numerous awards including First Prize in the Heritage Awards and Honourable Mention for Prose in the Cecilia Lamont Literary Contest. Portions of her novel *Everything's Coming Up Clover* were broadcast on the BBC and COAST Radio, Vancouver. The novel is based on Dora's observations as a care aide and an advocate for the elderly. Clover is a composite of the many eccentric and feisty women that Dora worked with as a care aide in Vancouver, British Columbia, Canada at Haro Park Centre.

Additional information available at www.dorapreston.com

MEMORIES OF DORA
From her friends, The Scribblers

Dora, the author, charmed us for many years with her Clover tales. Her legacy will live on in this gem of a book that is outrageous and laugh-out-loud funny with a heartbeat of warmth.

-Lara Sleath

At our weekly Scribblers meetings it was always a special treat when Dora read a Clover story. I can still hear her delightful Yorkshire accent as she regaled us with Clover's hilarious exploits. Dora had a truly zany brand of humour, guaranteed to make us laugh out loud. I had my favourite stories, which I never tired of hearing as Dora would read us newly edited versions.

It was like listening to treasured bedtime stories over and over. My very favourites were the writing classes with Mr. DeLamont, in which Clover wrote the absolute most over-the-top Gothic romances. I will never forget Deedry and Hades making hot, slippery love amidst banana peels in the banana plantation, or Aunt Skitsy's collection of live bats, attached to the wall with elastic bands. Both Dora and Clover will live forever in my heart.

-Susan Zuckerman

Clover, Give Over.

Even now, I swear I see her, this tiny bright-eyed woman with her tam and backpack. She was always, it seemed, in a hurry to get somewhere: a class, a meeting, a choir group or who-knows-where. Every Monday, I still see her sitting at that little table near the window at the V.C.C cafeteria before we would head off to Scribblers. I used to refer to her, affectionately, as Edith Bunker when I heard her singing in the bathroom. And at times when it seemed as if she would not or could not stop talking, I know, I am not the only one who would give anything to hear her sweet, distinctive voice again. To hear her say "Oh, give over," just one more time. And although she herself may be gone, hopefully, with this work, Clover, and her creator, will live forever.

-Don Peyton

I met Dora over twenty years ago at Francesca's *Wednesday Night Group* and through her writing came to appreciate her sense of humour, wit and charm. Lucky for me, when I joined *Scribblers* a few years ago, the camaraderie continued. Life had not always been easy for Dora but this didn't taint her attitude. She knew how to live one blessed day at a time. Her laugh was wide open, her zest for life, infectious. She was honest and accepting. These traits embroider her main character Clover, the eccentric troupe of side-kicks, and it stitches together the narrative of each lively story Dora penned.

-Laurel Mae Hislop

Because we lived in the same neighbourhood, Dora often rode home with me. I will never forget the Monday evening we left the Scribblers meeting in Vancouver's West End, an area I hadn't navigated for years, and I commented that I wasn't quite sure how to get to the Burrard Street Bridge. Without another word, Dora began to sing – a hilarious rhyming ditty about Old Man Denman chasing Miss Nicola, following Mr. Jervis who was a Bute until Mr. Thurlow attacked Mr. Burrard. She also had a song for remembering the cross-streets. Thus she found her way around Vancouver without a map. How I wish I had asked her to write the words down for us. Oh, Dora, we miss you and will always remember your wonderful sense of humour!

-Renate Ford

The last time I saw you I wanted to say goodbye, to tell you what a privilege it was to have known you, but I couldn't find the words. So I'm telling you now, Dora. Your unfailing positive attitude, your warm-hearted nature and, above all your amazing sense of humour, made you one of the most extraordinary people I have ever known. Goodbye Dora. I hope to see you soon.

-Rick Neal

Dora Preston was one of the most consistently cheerful people I have ever known. Yet her personal story, which she rarely spoke about, was not always so positive. I have many happy memories of her at Scribblers meetings and retreats on Mayne Island, always laughing and joking. On those special trips, she would wake us in the morning with a song in her wonderful singing voice, and get us to join her in the evenings to serenade the wild life in the cove nearby. Her stories of Clover had us all weeping with laughter. I think it is wonderful that a wider audience will have a chance to share in her ability to see the funny side of life.

-Dianne Maguire *Dry Land Tourist and other stories*

It was September 1989, West End Community Centre, Vancouver when I stepped into the washroom and a woman came in singing in a most lovely voice. I wondered who this happy person was and when I went into the West End Writer's meeting, there she was— Dora! I will always remember Dora for how she loved to sing. On

Mayne Island retreats she'd be up early trilling cheerfully until the rest of us got up. She was a talented humorist too, and whenever I taught a writing class, when it came to the humour writing, Dora was invited to come and share her stories. She always made us laugh!

-Ruth Kozak

Through the tales and innocence of Clover, the charm and vibrancy of this a-dora-ble character, Dora's spirit, zest and 'young-at-heart' personal style remains alive. Clover's adventures remind us that in our golden years, zealous youth can endure and rise above the anchors of time... life can begin again after 60.

-Beverley O'Neil

Driving Dora home at the end of our Scribblers weekly meetings was not only enjoyable but inspiring. She was never a silent passenger and her '*joie de vivre*' always transpired in our conversations, which could be intimate at times. She seemed to have an easy, down-to-earth solution to all problems. Her appreciation for little things in her daily life will remain an inspiration for what constitutes true happiness. Thank you, Dora, for your legacy.

-Diane Chouinard

When I think of Dora, and I still do from time to time, I have a whimsical image of all things English, tea, hats, songs of long ago, dress up, and Clover. She was songstress, funny girl, and confidante, kind soother of fragile ego, humorist and friend. I was writing a book about early Christianity. Not everyone in Scribblers agreed with the views expressed by some of my characters. When I drove Dora home from critique sessions, she would support those early Christian views. She distinguished between the good in the Christian faith and the evil done by some of its adherents. She may not have allowed others to know that the endearingly English part of her soul included traditional belief in the hereafter and its promise of reward for those who have faith. It was a privilege for me to be let in on those somewhat private beliefs. For my part, heaven is richer with her there.

-Wayne Gatley

The wit, charm and humour of Clover kept our Scribbler's group in giggles and outright snorts of laughter. Thank-you, Dora, for teaching me that no matter what your age, you can always bush-wack through the forest singing at the top of your lungs.

-Lea Ricketts

When I remember Dora, I hear her laughter, I see her elegant features and colourful clothing, and feel her genuine love of life despite her many hardships. She was a born comic and writer and I shall never forget her tales of the nursing home told with such wit and warmth. Dora wielded her brand of humour and persistence like a gentle sword. I will always miss her cheerful presence (although not her singing!)

-Val Gregory

When I first heard Dora read her tales of Clover's adventures in the senior's home, I thought she was practicing for an audition in a British sit-com. Her delivery was so lively and expressive, and her thick Yorkshire accent successfully transported me to a place with floral wallpaper, tea cosies and lots of tweed. In person, Dora was as cheerful and big-hearted as Clover and she always had a kind word to say about other people's writing. I miss her terribly, but I'm so happy that Dora lives on through Clover in this book.

-Mari Kane

Made in the USA
Charleston, SC
15 February 2014